THE THINGS WE HIDE

A creepy psychological thriller with a great twist

VANESSA GARBIN

THE BOOK FOLKS

Published by The Book Folks

London, 2024

This book is a work of fiction. Names, characters, businesses, organizations, places and events are either the product of the author's imagination or are used fictitiously. Any resemblance to actual persons, living or dead, events or locales is entirely coincidental. The spelling is Australian English.

ISBN 978-1-80462-255-1

www.thebookfolks.com

Also by Vanessa Garbin

WHAT WE DID LAST NIGHT

THE LIES I TOLD HIM

YOUR EVERY MOVE

THE STEPS WE TAKE

THEIR LITTLE SECRETS

NO FRIENDS OF MINE

FOR MY OWN GOOD

LIES WITHIN ME

Full details can be found at the back of this book.

www.thebookfolks.com

Prologue

My blood boils as I watch her go about her day, running errands and buying groceries without a care in the world.

She doesn't look sorry. But she should be.

Dismissing me like that, as though I don't exist. As though I don't have feelings. As though I'm not worth considering.

I'll *make* her sorry, that's what I'll do.

My knuckles bulge and whiten as I wrap my fingers around the steering wheel and squeeze hard, imagining what it would feel like to strangle the life out of her right here in this car park. Satisfying. Pleasurable even.

But of course I can't go around doing that in broad daylight. Some do-gooder will play the hero and perform a citizen's arrest. The police will be called and I'll get thrown into jail. Then after the cops do some digging, I'll be locked away for a very long time – maybe even for life.

No. Instead I breathe in deep and control my emotions, just like my online therapist taught me. Because my emotions are what almost got me into trouble last time.

I need to be more careful. I need to remind myself that I'm the one with the power.

I know her secret. Her dirty, filthy secret.

I just have to be patient.

Her time will come.

I'll take her down slowly. Cruelly.

Put her back in her place, where she belongs.

That will teach her to mess with me.

1

'Hi. I'm here for an interview about the waitressing position,' I say.

The young woman behind the counter studies my face, her expression blank, before her gaze flits down to my shirt, which is neatly tucked into my only pair of black slacks. She blinks slowly and inhales through her nose before finally making eye contact.

My stomach clenches with nerves. Hopefully she hasn't noticed the hastily mended tear in my shirt just below the collar. I would have preferred to have worn something new for the interview, but right now Matthew and I are behind on our rent and have hardly any food in the pantry and fridge, so a needle and thread to one of my old office shirts early this morning had to suffice.

Trendy music blasts through the speakers, filling the awkward few seconds it takes for the woman to say something.

'Take a seat over at the very back table, the reserved one. Gianni, the owner, will be with you shortly.'

'Thank you,' I say, smiling, but the woman keeps her face impassive and shifts her focus to a waiting customer.

The restaurant has been open for just over a year and is one of those swanky places that get away with selling cocktails for the price of a meal. As I make my way towards the back table and pass the busy, young and very attractive staff sporting clothes that I could never afford or even pull off, my confidence takes a dive.

But I tell myself that it's a bustling restaurant – tables are already starting to fill with customers at eleven-thirty in the morning. Despite the hour, expensive looking bottles of bubbly in shiny silver ice buckets sit on more than a few tables, and an array of upscale, artistic-looking cocktails steadily line the bar, ready to be ferried to waiting customers.

This place clearly needs more staff. Which hopefully means they need *me*. They might even ask me to start immediately. As in, today.

Feeling a little better, I try to picture myself showing customers to their tables, taking their orders with a smile, making polite chit-chat, and my stomach unclenches and begins to flutter with excitement. I might even make some decent tips, judging by the well-dressed clientele. At this point in our lives, every little bit will help.

I blink and straighten my back when a short and stocky man makes his way over to me. He's dressed in a white shirt which emphasises his olive skin, the sleeves rolled up to his elbows, and a pair of royal blue slacks that go with his eyes. It's hard not to notice the flash of gold around his neck, or the unnatural glow of his teeth when he smiles at me. He's a handsome man.

'Hello, Nadia is it?' he asks politely. 'I'm Gianni.'

I stand and shake his hand. 'Yes. Lovely to meet you.'

He nods and I don't miss the slight sigh of disappointment. He rests his hands on the back of the chair opposite mine and looks me right in the eye.

'Can I be straight with you?'

I nod and swallow thickly. This can't be good.

'We're a modern restaurant.' He waves a hand at the hip young staff carrying fancy dishes to their equally hip diners. 'And as such, it's a requirement that our staff fit the bill.'

I nod, my face beginning to warm. The worst part about this is that I'm at the very back of the restaurant, which means my walk of shame will be extra excruciating.

'Unfortunately – and I'm not knocking you because you're an attractive woman and seem like a nice person – but you don't have the vibe that I require my staff to have.' His cheeks swell with air and he blows it out in a noisy, vibrating puff. 'I'm really sorry. It's just business, that's all, nothing against you personally.'

My throat tightens with unexpected emotion but I quickly swallow it down and clear my throat.

'Okay. Well. Thank you for your time.' I smile brightly, doing my best to pretend that everything is okay even when it's not. To think I was foolish enough to have hoped for an immediate start.

He nods and smiles, but then his expression grows serious when his gaze falls on the sewed up tear below my collar.

'I tell you what, Nadia. For your troubles, take a seat and order what you like for lunch.' He waves one of the waitresses over, a pretty blonde with dark eyes, dressed head-to-toe in black. 'Ava here will sort you out,' he says, giving me a wink before telling Ava in a low murmur. 'It's on the house.'

Ava nods and gives me a wide smile. 'What can I get you, hon?'

Her friendliness brings another lump to my throat and I have to clear it to speak. 'I haven't looked at the menu yet,' I say, my face heating up as I slowly sink into my seat. I feel so out of place sitting here with my old clothes and bad haircut, being served by this much younger and gorgeously polished woman who looks like she stepped out of a fashion magazine.

'Are you a bubbly or a cocktail kind of girl?'

I shrug. 'I don't really know. I like everything.' I honestly can't remember the last time I had a cocktail.

'And what would you like to eat?'

I shrug again, my eyes stinging.

'Don't worry hon, I've got just the thing for you. Leave it with me.' She lightly touches my arm and sashays away to the beat of the music and disappears behind the bar.

I'm mortified and want to leave, but at the same time, my stomach is growling after seeing all the delectable food being served. So I blink back my tears and force myself to enjoy the moment. Because I might not get another meal like this for a while.

A wave of guilt washes over me to think of Matthew stuck at home, sitting on his special chair, unable to do much. But then I remember all the bottles of alcohol he wasted our precious rent money on, and the guilt soon fritters away. I'm allowed a treat, surely. And I haven't had a drink in such a long time.

Ava returns with an elegant looking rose-pink cocktail with tiny pale flowers floating in it.

'This is the *Flowers for a Flower* cocktail,' she says with a wink. 'Your food is coming right up.'

I thank her profusely. After she's gone, I reach for the delicate stem of the glass and bring the drink to my lips.

Heaven. That's the only word to accurately describe the delicate floral flavours swimming around my tongue right now.

I sigh and set the drink back down.

Somebody at the table next to me clears their throat.

'That looks good.' A woman with closely cropped dark hair and deep brown eyes smiles at me, before draining her champagne flute.

'It's lovely,' I say.

Now I'm embarrassed, because it's clear that this woman heard the exchange between me and Gianni and knows that I'm eating here only because of Gianni's guilty conscience and sense of charity.

'I hope I'm not being intrusive,' she says, opening up her handbag. 'But I couldn't help overhear you speaking with the owner about a job.'

'Unfortunately, I didn't get it,' I say with a sigh, and take a sip of my drink.

She tilts her head to the side as though appraising me. 'I might just have the right position for you.'

My heart skips on its beat. 'What kind of job?'

'Real estate. I know someone, my brother actually, who runs a firm over at Port Coogee. Gorgeous views.'

My heart sinks. 'I have zero experience with real estate.'

She waves my pessimistic words away. 'You don't need experience. Jace likes to train his staff himself.'

'Really?'

'Really. Here's my card. I'll have a chat with him in the next hour or so and see if I can get you an interview. Shoot me a text with your name and I'll get back to you before the end of the day.'

I take the card and glance at it quickly. It's a simple business card, just a name and contact details, nothing to hint at what she does for a living. Perhaps she works at the agency.

'Thanks, Dawn. I really appreciate it.'

Ava returns with a platter loaded with an assortment of delicious-looking bites. Prawns, arancini, a small pot of herbed linguini pasta, olives, cold meats, a selection of cheeses and some sliced bread.

'Everything is house made, including the pasta, bread and the cured meats. Gianni owns a farm and vineyard down south.' She lightly touches my arm again. 'Enjoy, sweetie.'

'Thank you,' I say, my voice hoarse with emotion.

Dawn clears her throat again.

I meet her gaze and gesture at the food. 'There's no way I'm going to be able to eat all of this. Would you like to help me at least make a dent in it?'

She laughs. 'I'm sorry, but I have an appointment with a client in fifteen. But remember to message me.' She glances again at the food, widening her eyes for effect, then grins. 'Enjoy.'

I smile and take a sip of my cocktail before picking up a fork and piercing a prawn doused in garlic and parsley. As soon as it's in my mouth, it practically melts against my tongue it's so tender, and I groan. No wonder Gianni's restaurant is doing so well.

I try a little bit of everything and can't fault any of it. But I'm soon full, and the dish looks barely touched, which makes me feel awful for wasting it all.

Gianni glances at me from behind the bar and smiles, before disappearing into the kitchen and returning with a container.

'We usually don't do this in our restaurant, but for you today, we do.' He hands me the container.

'Thank you,' I say, not feeling one bit of shame as I begin scraping food into the takeaway container. I'm too happy to feel embarrassed anymore because Dawn has given me a second chance at getting a job, and I'll be bringing Matthew home an amazing feed that he'll love.

I press the lid down on the near-bursting container and enjoy the rest of my cocktail.

Before I leave, I thank Gianni profusely and wave at Ava, before stepping outside into the warm sunshine.

Once I'm sitting in my car, I message Dawn with my name and email address, then start the engine and head for home.

Now all I have to do is wait.

2

A week later

'Wish me luck,' I say, slinging a brown handbag over my shoulder.

My husband stares me up and down and smiles sadly.

'You look beautiful,' he says, sounding depressed about it. 'With that skirt on, you'll get the job; one hundred percent.'

'Um, I'd like to think I'll get the job based on my brains, not my body.'

Matthew quirks a single brow and rubs at his unshaven chin. 'If the boss is a bloke, then you've got the job, trust me,' he says bitterly. 'This is the way the world works.'

'In that case, maybe I should have worn this skirt for Gianni,' I mutter.

'Who?' Matthew narrows his gaze at me with suspicion.

I roll my eyes because I told him about Gianna last week when I brought him the doggy-bag container of food. 'Nobody.'

He grunts in response and swears beneath his breath, shaking his head.

'You shouldn't joke about that sort of thing. Wearing a skirt like that is asking for trouble with that fruitcake on the loose.' He shakes his head. 'You know they still haven't taken down his Instagram page? No matter how many times I've reported it they still allow him to keep posting photos and crap about you.' He shakes his head and glares at me. 'How are you okay about it?'

I stiffen, like I always do whenever Matthew brings my stalker up. Not only do I not like to be reminded of the fact that someone is out there posting old photos of me on the internet, I also don't like the dark side it brings out of my husband. He's almost as obsessed with the stalker as the stalker is with me.

'Trust me, I'm not okay about it. And I get that you're worried about me. But I need to be able to go out and find a job. If I don't, we're going to end up on the streets.'

'But it's not safe for you. He could be following you.'

'I know that. Thanks for reminding me.' My hands are trembling now as I check that I've got everything I need in my handbag. 'But what else do you expect me to do, Matt? If I let my fear rule, we won't have any rent money.'

'But he's posting every day now and–'

'Just delete the app from your phone. That's the only way I'm able to block it out and move on,' I say.

'But he's posting photos of *you*, of my beautiful wife,' says Matt. 'I just can't ignore that.'

'I know. But at least it's only old photos. Nobody would recognise me from back then. And the photos are so blurry.' I force a grin and try to inject some lightness into the dark mood between us. 'I doubt anybody is interested in an old photo of a teenage girl dissecting a rat for science class.'

Matthew slams his fist against the table so hard the empty glass in front of him jumps. I do too. 'I said, don't joke about it. This is serious.'

I bite down on my bottom lip, to keep it from trembling. Although it's been six months since his work accident, Matthew's complete change in personality still shocks and saddens me. He used to be so upbeat, like a beam of sunshine streaming through the heavy curtains of life, brightening up the bleaker moments. But ever since he hurt his lower back and is pretty much confined to a specially-cushioned chair all day – one we had to order from a seniors' website, much to Matthew's disgust – he's more like a dark cloud that cloaks everything and everyone around him in gloom.

I raise my palms. 'Okay. I'm sorry. I know I shouldn't joke about it. But the police can't help me so what else can I do about it? If I take it too seriously, I'll be scared to leave the house.' I soften my voice. 'And I need to be able to go out and get work, Matt. We need this money.'

He shrugs and picks at a chip in the wooden tabletop.

'So you're not going to wish me luck?' I ask.

Matthew regards me with hard eyes, but then something inside of him softens, and his shoulders slump.

'I'm sorry, Nards,' he says. 'I just hate not working anymore.' He reaches for the glass on the table but swears when he sees that it's empty, his gaze seeking the bourbon bottle which is now gone.

'I threw it out. The whole lot. You've got to stop drinking. It's changing you.'

Matthew sighs, his hands clenching into fists. 'I need it. For the pain. Just until I get the operation. If I ever bloody get it.'

I sigh, force a smile, and bend down to press my lips to his stubbly cheek.

'And that's why I'm going for this job. It's going to pay for the surgery you need. And then you'll be back to your old self.'

'You shouldn't have to, though. My boss should be paying for this. I should be covered by workers' comp.' He shakes his head and snorts. 'I used to lug huge stone benchtops and cabinetry into houses all day every day for them, and yet they think I did this at home mowing the lawn. Greedy bastards.' Matthew automatically reaches for the empty glass again and then recoils when he remembers that there's no more booze to drink.

'Look, I'm going to be late. I need to go.' My stomach twists with nerves as I jangle our car keys. We've been sharing a car for the past couple of months after I had to sell mine to pay for last month's rent. It's not as though Matthew can drive in his condition anyway.

'I'll see you in an hour or so,' I say from the door of our apartment.

Matthew waves a hand in my direction but refuses to look me in the eye.

'Good luck, Nadia,' he says, his head down, and sounding so broken I could cry.

As I walk out the door, I hear his phone beep and think about that friend of his he met on an Alcoholics Anonymous forum. Sometimes I wish that I'd never convinced Matthew to join that group, because now it seems that he's drinking even more.

But as I get into the car, I banish all traces of negative thoughts and concerns and instead try to direct my thoughts towards more positive things. Like this job opportunity.

By the end of today, I might be lucky enough to be employed again. And who knows, after saving enough money to get Matthew the operation, he might not need the Alcoholics Anonymous forum anymore.

And maybe, just maybe, our lives will take a turn for the better.

3

The real estate office is at the Port Coogee marina. As soon as I get out of the car, I inhale deeply, taking in the salty air, and allow the morning sun to warm my face while seagulls soar and shriek at me from a perfectly blue sky.

Dawn was right about the gorgeous views. It would be incredible to work here every day. I could grab fish and chips on my lunch break, take a long walk and admire all the pretty houses and apartments in the area, or simply sit on one of the many park benches and stare out at the sailboats bobbing along the shimmering surface of the ocean.

But, of course, that's not the main reason for wanting this job.

My husband and I are getting so far behind on our rental payments that I'm worried we'll get an eviction notice soon and end up living out of our car. And I doubt sleeping in a 1994 Nissan Pulsar will do wonders for Matthew's bad back.

Of course, we *were* doing fine, well, maybe not fine, but we were at least making ends meet up until around two months ago, even with Matthew having already been at home for over four months with his injured back. But then I lost my job as a receptionist when my boss died of a sudden heart attack and his distraught wife decided it was best to shut down his mechanical workshop for good.

But now I'm here, ready to enter the office, my stomach churning with anxiety as I'm about to be interviewed for the position of a real estate agent of all things.

I've tried applying for every office job under the sun, office jobs, amusement park ride operator, retail assistant, cleaning jobs, and lastly waitressing – which I'd previously vowed never to return to after spending my late teen years doing exactly that, and not enjoying it one bit – but for some reason I keep missing out. Maybe they can smell the desperation on me. I'm sure I reek of it.

But hopefully today is different and I'll walk away with a job offer.

Just as I'm about to enter the office, someone opens the door and steps out.

'Dawn,' I say, offering her a nervous smile. 'Thanks for this.'

'Oh hey, Nadia,' she says, smiling brightly at me and holding the door open. 'I'm off to work. Best of luck.'

'Thanks. So you don't work here?'

'No,' she says laughing before grimacing comically. 'My brother and I would kill each other if we had to work side by side. No. I'm a physio for an aged care centre.'

'Oh,' I say, feeling a little disappointed that she doesn't work at the agency. I'd already envisioned us sharing an after-work bottle of wine at one of the many marina restaurants.

'Don't look so nervous. Jace doesn't bite. You're in good hands.' She glances down at her phone and yelps. 'Ah, I'm late. Good luck!'

She hurries away before I can say thank you, leaving behind a cloud of perfume that tickles my nose.

The office is neat and tidy, more spacious than it looks from the outside. Along the walls hang framed awards for high sales achievements. A twenty-something guy mans the reception desk. He smiles up at me and adjusts his glasses when he raises his eyes from the computer screen in front of him.

'Hello. You must be Nadia?'

'Yes,' I say. 'I have an interview at nine-thirty.'

He nods. 'Jace will be out in just a moment. He's on a call.' He flicks a glance at the cream couch across the room. 'Please take a seat. He won't be long.'

'Thank you.'

The couch is made from of leather and is butter-soft to touch. As I relax against it and stare up at all the framed awards on the walls, I dream of the day Matt and I can buy furniture as luxurious as this for our home. How wonderful would that be? To go out and purchase things because they are beautiful, not because they fit the budget.

'Hello, Nadia?'

A tall, incredibly good-looking man in his thirties, dressed in an expensive navy suit, waves a hand across my line of vision from across the room.

I blink and immediately spring from the couch.

'Yes. I'm sorry,' I say, heat rising to my cheeks.

'Not at all,' the man says, smiling warmly. 'Come through to my office where we can have a nice chat. I'm Jace, by the way.' He allows me to enter first, then he closes the door behind him and gestures to the seat opposite his desk.

I sit down.

Jace's office is decorated tastefully in a black and white theme, but framed coloured photographs of himself and a blonde woman at various adventurous holiday locations add warmth and colour to the room.

Jace follows my gaze and grins. 'My stunning wife,' he says, proudly.

Lucky wife, I think, as I imagine what it would be like to be whisked away to such exotic destinations. Matthew and I can't even afford a road trip down south to stay at a caravan park.

In all the photos, Jace's wife is beaming a huge smile. And why wouldn't she?

But I shouldn't be so quick to assume that it's Jace paying for these trips. His wife could be the big breadwinner and perhaps Jace is the one being whisked away.

'So,' he says, drumming his desk with his hands. 'I'll be frank with you. We've been through three people the past two months. Given them the job, spent time training them, only to have them up and leave. So...' He leans forward and looks me dead in the eye.

I can't help but notice how gorgeous Jace's dark brown eyes are. As I stare into them, his aftershave clouds my head, and my cheeks grow warm as I think about how handsome he is. I clear my dry throat. I could use a glass of water right about now.

'So,' he repeats. 'Are you willing to commit, Nadia? It's one hell of a ride, with plenty of ups and downs, but... the ups are–' He leans back in his chair and gestures to the framed photographs. 'The ups are worth it.'

Okay, so it *is* Jace doing all the whisking.

He raises his brows and grins. 'Plus, I buy breakfast for the staff every Friday morning. Whatever you like. There's a cute café around the corner that makes an amazing eggs benedict and their coffee is worth dying for.'

Jace's silly grin sets me at ease and all the tension in my body unfurls.

'Okay, now I'm totally onboard,' I say.

Jace laughs and I do too. He's even more attractive when he laughs. Now I know why the three people before me left after only a few weeks. They probably couldn't concentrate on their work with this man around.

'The only problem...' I say, fiddling with the strap of my bag. 'Is that I don't have any experience in real estate.'

'Well as I mentioned, we offer full training. If you're willing to learn, we'll teach you everything you need to know.'

We spend some time talking through the role and a bit of history about the firm. Jace is obviously very pleased with how well the company is doing and how far they have come.

'So, what do you think? The job is yours if you want it.'

'Yes,' I say with a firm nod. 'I want this job very much.'

He stands and claps his hands together.

'Wonderful. I'll have Adam at the front desk give you an employment package. It'll have all the forms you need to fill out – there's an option to do it all online if you feel more comfortable doing it that way – as well as some information on our company and how we work.' He thrusts his right hand out. 'Welcome aboard, Nadia. I have a great feeling about you,' he says.

I rise to my feet and take his hand, and the moment my palm connects with his, a bolt of warmth shoots through me like electricity.

Matthew and I haven't been able to have sex since his injury. And although I've offered to help him in other ways, the medication he's on seems to have zapped him of any desire to be intimate with me.

My physical attraction to Jace is both surprising and horrifying. I've never been attracted to someone on first sight. It takes a lot of talking and getting to know someone before I can feel anything physical for them. That's how it happened with Matthew and me. Once I got to know how funny and kind he was, I fell head over heels for him. The fact that he's good-looking is a bonus. Five years on I still feel so much love for him. Even though it's been tough these past six months.

'Thank you,' I say to Jace, ending the handshake as quickly as possible. 'You won't be disappointed.'

'That's good to hear,' he says, coming around the desk to get the door for me. 'Welcome to the team.'

'Thank you,' I say again, feeling a surge of hope, and joy. But on my way out, the strap of my fifteen-dollar handbag, which is already broken and held together by a safety pin, gets caught on the door handle and completely snaps. Jace meets my gaze and my cheeks prickle with heat as I wrap the broken strap around the bag and pray to be swallowed alive by a sinkhole.

'Don't worry,' he says with a wink. 'You'll be able to replace that bag with a nice fat commission in no time, Nadia.'

I release a shaky laugh. 'I hope so,' I say, hating the desperation in my voice.

'Don't look so worried. All of us started at the bottom. We will fully train you. Trust me.' He gives me a wink that sets my heart a flutter. 'You'll be on top before you know it.'

After he lets Adam at the front desk know that I'm joining the team, Jace disappears into his office without a backward glance. Good. It's all business on Jace's end. Maybe that thing he said about being on top wasn't innuendo but just my ridiculous imagination. The lightning bolt of attraction I felt for him only moments ago was just a me-thing. A one off, probably because of the lack of intimacy in my life. That's all.

Because the last thing I need is to develop a ridiculous crush on my boss.

I'm here to earn money.

Money for my husband's operation.

And I'll do anything to make sure that he gets it.

4

That night, Matthew and I celebrate by heading out to the marina to have fish and chips by the sea. I bring along blankets and several pillows to ensure that Matt is as comfortable as possible.

Once we're settled on a park bench which offers stunning ocean views, our warm parcels on our laps, I whip out a mini bottle of non-alcoholic bubbly and two plastic cups. I found it in the bargain bin priced at only two dollars at the local bottle shop because the label was half torn off.

'Let's celebrate,' I say, my smile too wide and my voice too loud. I guess I'm trying to inject some cheer into my husband, who has looked miserable ever since I arrived home to tell him the good news.

Matthew smiles, but the warmth doesn't quite meet his eyes. I know that it hurts him not being able to contribute financially, and I know it's the reason why he didn't react to my announcement with as much enthusiasm as I'd hoped.

But I appreciate the effort he's made this evening, dressing in a smart, collared shirt that he hasn't worn since my sister's wedding in Melbourne two years ago. He's even combed his hair and had a shave.

The warm rays of the setting sun give my husband's skin a healthy golden hue. Before the back injury, Matt was always outdoors, either fishing or gardening or going on long walks – taking me along with him, of course, which blessed us both with a year-round tan.

Now, however, because he rarely leaves the house, his skin has turned as pale and as pasty as the dull walls of our rental.

He takes the tiny bottle from my hands and makes a 'pop' sound with his mouth as he unscrews the little lid.

I laugh and he joins me, which is a lovely surprise. Matt's finally warming up. My good mood has become as infectious as I'd hoped.

We tap our cups together then take sips. The bubbles fizz on my tongue pleasantly. Though I wish it were alcoholic, it's not terrible.

Matt grimaces a little. I know he'd rather it was a proper drink but there's no way I'm going to give him that. The last thing I need is for my husband to go on another one of his drinking benders. And anyway, we don't have the money for alcohol right now.

'I suppose we'll be able to afford the real stuff soon,' he says.

And there it is. The only problem this new job presents is the fact that Matthew will have a steady supply of money to buy booze with.

I'll need to be crafty on pay day. Sort out the rent and the bills first, then stock up the pantry and fridge so that there isn't anything left for his vice. I'll be supportive, of course. It's not going to be easy for him to get on track.

'While you're home, I think it's best we keep the house alcohol free,' I say. Then I point out a pelican bobbing on the water, hoping to change the subject. I want to have a nice evening with my husband, not a frosty one. And I know from experience that talking about alcohol never ends well.

Matt sets his cup down carefully on the bench between us and opens his parcel of fish and chips. I do the same.

'This is so good,' I say, as I bite into a hot chip, still feeling the buzz from hearing Jace tell me that I got the job.

'Yeah,' says Matt, smiling genuinely this time as he stares across the water at a seagull as it dives for its own dinner in the sea in front of us. 'It's nice out here. We should get out of the house more often.'

Excitement fizzes through my veins, much like the bubbly drink. It's like I've travelled back in time and am sitting beside my husband of old.

'For sure. We could go on a picnic next weekend. Maybe Kings Park.'

Matt nods. 'I can make us my famous curried egg sandwiches.'

'Ooh, yum,' I say, blowing on a hot chunk of battered fish to cool it down. 'I'll chop up some cheeses and fruit. And we can pack a flask of coffee.'

Matt's face brightens and he opens his mouth to speak, but he's interrupted when someone calls out from behind us.

'Nadia!'

I turn in my seat and crane my neck to see Jace striding towards us. He must have only just left the office as he is still wearing the same navy suit from our interview.

'Hi,' says Jace, extending a hand to Matthew, who awkwardly wipes his salt and grease covered palm on his jeans, before shaking it. 'I'm Jace, your wife's new boss.'

'Oh, okay,' says Matthew, withdrawing his hand. He doesn't offer his name. I can tell by the look on his face that he doesn't like Jace one bit. Perhaps he didn't appreciate the 'your wife's new boss' part.

'Well,' Jace says, 'I don't want to spoil a romantic evening, so I'll leave you to it.' He nods at Matt then turns to me. 'I'll email you some time over the weekend – just some basic information about the company and the kind of clientele we work with. But otherwise, I'll be seeing you at 9am on Monday morning, sharp.'

I'm not sure why, but I give him a little salute, soldier-like, to which his eyes sparkle with amusement.

'Goodbye, Nadia,' he says, before he turns and walks away.

Matts face screws up when I meet his gaze.

'What's with the salute?' he asks, rolling his eyes before he takes a bite of fish.

I shrug. 'I don't know. I get nervous talking to people I don't know well. You should know,' I say, and give him a knowing look.

I shake my head and smile at the memory. I was so nervous when I first met Matt that I knocked his beer to the floor when I stuck my hand out for him to shake.

But Matt's smile has gone down with the setting sun, and I'm left sitting beside my husband feeling cold and alone.

5

My first week flies by so fast that I'm surprised when Jace pops his head around the door to my office and tells me that it's time for breakfast.

'My shout on Fridays, remember?'

I nod. However, when we leave, I notice that none of the other staff members are joining us.

'Are the others meeting us there?' I ask as Jace and I leave the office and step out onto the paved street which leads us towards the strip of cafés and restaurants.

A cool, gentle breeze tickles my hair and gives me goosebumps. Although it's still autumn, the air has gotten dramatically cooler these past few days. Or maybe it's because I'm out of the suffocating confines of our stuffy apartment and exposed to all this fresh, sea air.

'Unfortunately not all of us can leave the office and since it's your first week the others have kindly offered to hold the fort while I treat you to your first company breakfast.'

I smile, but my stomach flutters with unease. Although I would never entertain any kind of funny business with him, I find it difficult to be around Jace without making a bit of a fool out of myself. On my first day, Monday morning, we accidentally brushed hands when he passed me a file and of course my face turned bright red. It's ridiculous. I'm thirty-two years old, not sixteen.

When we arrive at the café which boasts a stunning view over the marina, we are greeted by a blonde woman who nods towards a booth at the very front with uninterrupted views.

Seagulls caw and the water flutters gently against the moored sailboats and when Jace excuses himself to speak to the woman who greeted us, I allow myself to relax against the soft booth seats and become mesmerised by the rhythmic bobbing of the boats.

It seems surreal that that a little over a week ago I was sitting at the dining table in our apartment scouring the internet for jobs and now I'm here, in this cute little café in Port Coogee, looking out onto the stunning Indian Ocean.

By the end of today, my first pay will be getting transferred into my bank account. Into our shared bank account. And slowly, over time, if we are frugal and put some of our money away, Matthew will be able to get his much-needed back operation and we can start anew. Get a new place to live. Maybe even put a deposit on our own place.

Matt wants to eventually move to the country. His grandmother lives about three hours away, south of Perth, on a large rural property just outside a small coastal town called Saltbush Bay. She once told him that she'd left the property to him in her will now that his parents have both passed away. But Matt loves his grandmother dearly and of course he'd rather she live to two hundred, than die just so that he can inherit her property.

Sometimes Matt hints at moving in with Maida now, while she's still alive. But if our wedding was anything to go by – she sobbed in Matt's arms and told me that I had stolen her Matty boy – I can't imagine she'd welcome me into her own home with open arms.

'I've ordered for the both of us.'

I look up, jolted from my thoughts. Jace smiles down at me, the gentle breeze ruffling his blond fringe. 'I hope you don't mind.'

'Oh... not at all.' I actually do mind, a little. But I'll let it go this one time only because he's being so generous.

He takes a seat across from me and the morning light warms his dark eyes, turning them a rich chocolate colour. Jace grins when he catches me staring and I look away and think about Matthew, and how he used to look like that before his back injury.

Matt's eyes used to sparkle with the same vitality and his smile had the power to change your mood in an instant. He used to practically bounce out of bed and dance his way into the kitchen to make his morning coffee. Then when I got up, he'd slide his arms around me from behind and press his lips against my neck in a way that sometimes made us late for work.

I miss that Matt. And I cannot wait for us to be like that again.

'What's on your mind?' Jace asks. 'You look far away.'

I tuck a lock of hair behind my ear. 'Oh, it's nothing.'

Jace's eyes turn serious. 'You can tell me anything, Nadia. What is said at breakfast, stays at breakfast.' He mimes zipping his lips and I can't help but smile.

I shrug. 'I was just thinking about my husband Matt.'

'The guy I met the other evening?' Jace grimaces slightly. 'Now please tell me if I'm overstepping here, but I got the feeling he wasn't too happy about the job... am I right?'

'Kind of.' A fierce urge to protect Matthew surges from within. 'But it's only because he wishes he was the one out working. He'd rather it be him and doesn't like that I have the responsibility of being the sole breadwinner.'

Our coffees arrive. 'Almond latte. How did you know?'

Jace taps his temple. 'I'm not just a pretty face, you know – I notice things.' He grins then shrugs. 'When Adam took your coffee order yesterday, I overheard and took note.'

'Thank you. It's very sweet of you.'

'My pleasure.' He studies me from across the table, his eyes serious. 'Now tell me more about your husband and why he isn't working.'

I take a sip of coffee then relax into my seat. 'Matthew has a bad back. He needs an operation. An expensive one.'

Jace grimaces. 'That's rough. I take it there's no workers' compensation?'

'No. His boss is being a–' I bite my lip.

'A stingy arsehole about it?'

'One hundred percent. He believes that Matt hurt his back at home. Which is ridiculous seeing as he was lifting items that weigh over thirty kilos on a daily basis.' Jace says nothing in response and I shift in my seat, uncomfortable now under such intense scrutiny. Maybe he thinks I'm complaining too much. 'But it's fine. I have this job now, which means a regular income, and we are planning on saving for the operation, so...' My words die away.

Jace frowns then clears his throat. 'I can imagine that will take a while though.'

I blush. 'I know. I don't expect to be earning top dollar yet. Printing flyers isn't exactly going to earn me millions.'

Jace shrugs. 'Hey, we all have to start somewhere.' Then he smiles softly and nods. 'You'll get there eventually.'

The food arrives.

Eggs benedict. Luckily, I love eggs benedict. Matthew made this for me on the first morning of our honeymoon.

'Try it.' Jace nods at the delectable-looking plate of food in front of me. 'And prepare to be amazed. The best eggs benedict in the country.'

Under Jace's watchful gaze, I pick up my cutlery and try my best to look elegant as I cut into my food and put a forkful of it into my mouth. Wow. The perfectly poached eggs and the delicious hollandaise sauce melt together on my tongue beautifully, making my heart sing.

Chewing my food, I nod at Jace and offer a thumbs up, hoping that he can't tell that I'm blushing underneath my makeup.

He smiles and begins eating and I'm thankful that he's no longer watching me so closely.

I'm not sure why being in Jace's presence makes me so nervous, but I suppose Matthew has been so off me, so off sex, so off... everything really, except talking to his online friends on the Alcoholics Anonymous app, that Jace's attention is a little bit confronting. I've almost forgotten how flattering, but also disconcerting it is to hold a man's complete and undivided attention.

'It's really good,' I say, after I've swallowed my mouthful of food and taken another sip of my coffee.

'It's it,' he says. He takes a large bite and rests his chin on his hands while he chews and watches me closely again.

'Do I have something on my face?' I ask, feeling annoyed at his scrutiny, and also a little paranoid that I do actually have food on my face. I pick up my napkin and dab at my lips.

'No.' He shakes his head lightly. 'I was just thinking about your... situation.' He takes a sip of his coffee and clears his throat. 'I think I can help.'

'You've already helped enough. You hired me.'

'I know. But... I mean *real* help, not the going-award-rate kind of help. I want to offer you something I normally don't do for newcomers. But I haven't met someone in your kind of predicament.' He shrugs. 'You need help, and I can offer it.'

I rest my cutlery against my plate and raise my palms. 'If you're offering some kind of company loan, I don't want it. We're in debt enough as it is.' I sigh. 'We haven't been able to pay our rent lately, so... yeah, more debt is something that we don't need.' I put a hand to my lips, embarrassed that I just revealed how dire our situation is in front of my new boss.

Jace lightly slaps the table with his palms. 'Okay, so all the more reason for you to say yes to my offer.'

'Yes to what exactly?' I ask, my voice laced with caution.

'This weekend I'm doing a home open down south in Busselton. It's a beachside mansion, high ten mills. I've sold for this customer in the past. He's a man of strange tastes... a bit of a character, but he keeps my wife happy with the commissions I'm earning.'

'Ten *million* dollars?'

He nods and flashes me a grin.

'Come down with me for the weekend.' He slaps the table again. 'You can watch me work my magic, and, if you help me to secure a sale during that time, then I'll give you...' He pauses, then his gaze grows intense. 'I'll give you half my commission.'

I don't respond. Because one, there is no way that Matt will want to be left alone at home on his own for an entire weekend, and two, I highly doubt that Jace will give me, a complete newbie, half of the very fat commission he'd get for selling a ten-million-dollar home. Still, my heart races at the thought of potentially earning that kind of money in a single weekend.

'This is a great opportunity for you, Nadia. I don't do this for just anyone.' He relaxes against the back of his booth seat and nods. 'I see potential in you. Huge potential.'

From printing flyers? I highly doubt it. Maybe he can see the money hungry glint in my eyes.

'I can't accept your offer,' I say. 'As kind as it is. It's your sell and your money.' I sigh hopelessly. 'And I'm not sure that my husband will be okay with me disappearing for an entire weekend. He needs me around to help him with day to day stuff.'

'Surely he can ask a friend to help him. And don't worry about me, I sell properties for high prices all over this marina. Have you seen the houses around here? Nadia, I make *a lot* of money. This will not hurt me. And the company will pay for all the accommodation and other expenses along the way so it won't cost you a cent.' He raises his brows. 'So? What do you say? I'm sure Matt will be pleased when he hears about the potential commission.'

'He might be...' I say, mulling over my decision.

Who am I kidding? If it means being able to pay the overdue rent and keep a roof over our heads, and pay for his operation, Matt will likely pack my bags for me and push me out the door. In a normal situation he wouldn't be so eager to let me go away on a work weekend with a male colleague, but in this case, with the current delicate circumstance we're in, I'd say he might react differently.

'So if you sell this property, this weekend, you're saying, that if I help you, I'll receive half the commission?'

He nods. 'I'm a man of my word. And I believe it'll be an easy sell. We have a curated list of clients for properties like this one. Trust me, you'll be walking away with enough money to pay for your husband's operation, and more, by Sunday afternoon.'

I shake my head, unable to believe my good fortune.

'Then I guess I'll have to say yes,' I say. 'But I want to earn this. You need to let me roll up my sleeves and properly help you sell this mansion.'

'Of course. You strike me as the kind of person who doesn't take handouts, and I respect that. This isn't a handout. This is simply business. Work.' He smiles, and it lights up his eyes. 'You can trust me.'

'Okay,' I say, nodding, butterflies stirring my stomach.

'Now, eat up because we need to make plans. I want to leave just after lunch to beat the Friday afternoon traffic madness. I'll have reception book you a room at the same hotel I'm staying at.'

The fluttering in my stomach intensifies at the thought of staying overnight in the same hotel as Jace. I'm one hundred percent sure that Matthew is not going to be happy about that. But it doesn't make sense for us to stay at separate hotels when we're going to be spending so much time together. And besides, the company probably has some kind of deal with the hotel. Anyway, once he figures out how much money I may potentially earn this weekend, he probably won't mind so much.

I do the maths in my head and gasp when I work out my share of the commission. Split down the middle, if Jace is true to his word, I'll walk away with over one hundred thousand dollars for just one weekend of work.

This has to be a dream.

'So are you definitely in?' Jace asks.

I smile at him.

'One hundred percent.'

6

After we finish eating breakfast, Jace immediately dismisses me from work to give me enough time to pack, and also to allow me time to convince Matthew that this is an opportunity I can't say no to. So basically all I did this morning was fold a few flyers and then eat a delicious eggs benedict and now I've got the rest of the day off. It almost seems too good to be true. I drive home, feeling as though I'm floating inside a bubble of joy.

Of course, when I pull up at our apartment block, my bubble of joy bursts.

When I met Matthew, one of the things I immediately loved about him was the fact that he wasn't one of those jealous types who thinks he owns his partner. He believed, like me, that a successful relationship is two souls who *choose* to be together. We are here, in this marriage, by choice and our love for one another.

But since he got laid off at work, he's changed, and has started exhibiting possessive behaviours. Once, when I was still working at the mechanical workshop, I stayed behind at the end of the day for a fellow employee's birthday do. Stan had turned sixty, so it was a special birthday, and our boss had put on a sausage sizzle along with some wine and beer. It was fun. I had a barbequed sausage in a piece of bread and a small glass of white wine, and didn't even stay long enough for the cake to be served, but I returned home to find Matt pacing the apartment and pointing a finger at me, accusing me of having an affair. It was as ludicrous as it was frightening.

Sometimes I wonder if it's the people he's talking to online. I don't know a thing about them and Matt spends several hours a day on there. There could be someone in his group chat that's influencing him. Poisoning his delicate mental state by sowing seeds of paranoia.

I draw in a deep breath and exhale noisily before getting out of the car. I take the stairs slowly, to give me time to mentally prepare my I'm-going-away-for-the-weekend-with-my-devilishly-handsome-boss speech.

The apartment door is ajar when I get to it, which is odd, and I open it slowly, and enter with caution.

'Matthew?' I call out.

He's not in his special chair, but I hear the shower running, which I suppose is a good thing. He normally waits for me to help him to get into the shower, because he worries he'll fall. Perhaps this is a sign he's beginning to feel positive about our situation.

Tossing my bag on the couch, I spend the next few minutes tidying the house, noting happily that there aren't any signs of alcohol use. I sniff the glass on the coffee table, but find no telltale grainy scent. People say you can't smell vodka, but I can.

But as I'm loading the dishes into the sink, I can't help but notice two glasses drying on the rack. I touch them. They're still wet, which means he only just washed them. I pick them up and smell them, of course I can only smell a faint hint of apple-scented dishwashing liquid but I freeze when I notice a tiny smudge of pink lipstick on the rim of one of the glasses. I only wear nude lipstick as the brighter colours wash me out, which means this smudge belongs to another woman.

'Hey,' Matthew calls out behind me, just as I wipe the offending lipstick away with the dishcloth. 'What are you doing home so early?'

'Hi,' I say, turning around and leaning back against the sink. 'Did you have a friend over?'

Matthew stops drying his hair with the towel. He's freshly shaven. That's something new. It's all adding up to something I never would have suspected of Matthew. Especially in his physical condition. Maybe the lack of sex between us is because he's getting it elsewhere.

'Yes. Remember? My first visit from the physio.' He smiles. 'At first, I thought she was a bossy old bag, but she gave me some home truths. She's older than us, but she's alright.' Matthew's eyes light up in a way that I haven't seen them do for a long time as he comes to stand in front of me. 'She made me realise that I can't sit around feeling sorry for myself forever. That I can shower, I can do small things for myself, and for you. And best of all I can make plans for our future.'

'I like where this is going,' I say, sliding my hands up and around his shoulders.

'Good. Because she made me believe that anything is possible.'

'Who *is* this woman?' I ask. Then I get on my tiptoes and pretend to look over his shoulder. 'And where did she put my husband?'

Matthew rolls his eyes. 'I haven't been that bad, have I?'

I raise my brows. 'Let's just say that seeing you like this... it's one of the best things that has happened to me today.'

He quirks a single brow and tugs me closer by the belt loops of my trousers. My heart flutters in response. I can smell the peppermint shampoo he uses, and the pine-scented soap he likes. He smells so good. And I wish that we could tear each other's clothes off in the heat of passion like we used to do.

'Now that you've got this job, I can finally see a future, good things on the horizon.' He looks me in the eye. 'You're amazing, Nadia. And I'm sorry that I don't tell you that enough anymore.'

'It's okay.'

'No. It's not okay. But it changes from this moment on.'

I smile up at him. 'Okay. Thank you.'

Matthew bends to peck me on my forehead and his body immediately tenses up.

'Hey, are you okay?'

He winces. 'I'm fine. After-effects of the physio, that's all.'

'Here, let me help you to your chair.'

Once I've got him seated, I sit opposite him on the couch. It squeaks and has a tear in the arm which we keep covered with one of Matt's grandmother's crocheted blankets, but it's comfortable.

'What are you smiling about?' he asks, half frowning, half smiling.

I cover my mouth and shake my head. 'It's nothing now, but I thought... when I walked in just now and found the glass on the dish rack with lipstick on it, I thought you might have been having an affair.'

Matthew laughs. 'No way. Why would I look elsewhere when I've got you?'

I laugh. Then I look at my watch and realise that I don't have much time between now and when Jace is picking me up.

'There's something I need to tell you.'

'Okay.' Matt eyes me suspiciously. 'It's something to do with work, isn't it? Don't tell me you've lost your job.'

I raise my palms. 'No, no. It's not that.'

'Then what are you looking so serious about?'

'Well, I've been offered a bit of an opportunity at work.'

Matt raises his brows. 'Already? You're not sleeping your way to the top, are you?' He laughs, but I can see the fine lines of concern gathering between his brows.

'Of course not. I've been offered to go down to a home open in Busselton. A beachside mansion that is selling for... wait for it... ten *million* dollars.'

Matt's eyes widen and he whistles softly. 'Imagine having so much money that you can afford a place like that?'

‘I know. And get this. I’ve been told that if I help to secure an offer over the weekend, that I get to keep half the commission.’ I make a steeple with my hands beneath my chin. ‘Guess how much that is?’

He shrugs. ‘I don’t know... ten grand? I don’t know how it all works.’

I take a deep breath and shuffle forward to the edge of the couch.

‘I’ll be taking home one hundred thousand dollars if the house sells. *One hundred grand*, Matt! In a single weekend.’

Matt’s stares at me, lost for words.

‘That’s amazing. So did you say yes?’

‘I did. But I wanted to double check with you first though. Because if you don’t think you can get by without me, then I’ll say no.’

‘No to a possible hundred grand? Are you mad?’

I smile and sigh with relief. ‘Okay, okay. I’ll do it.’ I get up and bend down to plant a kiss on Matt’s lips. ‘With this money we’ll be able to book your operation.’

Matthew rests his head against the back of the chair and closes his eyes. ‘It’s almost too good to be true, Nards. I almost don’t want to get too excited in case it doesn’t happen.’

I crouch in front of him and take his hand in mine, kissing his palm. He opens his eyes and cradles my face in his hand.

‘When do you leave?’ he asks.

‘Just after lunch. I’m getting picked up.’

‘Oh. Who’s driving?’

‘One of the agents,’ I say.

He nods and retracts his hand.

‘Is it your boss?’

‘Jace. Yeah. He said he sees a lot of potential in me.’

‘I’m sure he does,’ Matt mutters under his breath before rolling his eyes.

‘Don’t be like that. You said yourself it was a great opportunity and that I’d be stupid to say not to it.’

He sighs and meets my gaze. 'I know. I'm being a jerk. Just ignore me.'

I squeeze his hand then get up and plant a kiss on his forehead.

'I'm going to shower and pack. Can I make you something to eat beforehand?'

'No. I'm fine. The physio brought some muffins with her. We had tea.'

'Nice,' I say. I find the television remote and leave it with him so that he can watch the telly while I'm getting ready.

It's not until I'm in the shower that I realise something. If they did truly drink tea, why are whisky glasses on the rack and not mugs or teacups?

I close my eyes and allow the warm water to stream into my face. I've got to stop looking for trouble where there is none. I'm sure there's some explanation for the whisky glasses. I rub a blob of shampoo into my hair and lather away the doubt.

I need to focus on Busselton and the sale of this house.

That fat commission is going to help us get back on track to living our lives the way we've always imagined.

Happily ever after.

7

I drag my weekend bag, which is packed with clothes that I'm still unsure about, into the living room. What exactly does one wear to a ten-million-dollar property showing?

The smooth rumble of a sports engine pulling into the apartment car park sends a shiver down my spine.

Seconds later I get a message from Jace.

I'm here.

I look at Matthew, who's seated at the dining table doing a crossword, a pillow wedged behind his back for support.

'It's time for me to go.'

He nods and carefully eases himself to stand before shuffling towards me and taking me into his arms.

'I love you, Nadia. I'm going to miss you.'

I carefully wrap my arms around his waist. 'I'm going to miss you too and I can't wait to come home on Sunday night with good news, fingers crossed.'

He smiles down at me, his eyes sparkling with hope, looking very much like the man I first met.

'You'll get that commission.' He grins. 'You wanna know how I know? Because nobody will be able to say no to anything you're selling. You're the most beautiful woman in the world.'

'Let's hope so,' I say with a chuckle, and rest my head against his chest.

The steady drum of Matthew's heartbeat soothes me. I wish that I could stay right here, in my husband's arms instead of going away to Busselton. Seeing Matt so hopeful like this, so like the old Matt, it's like having to leave him after only just being reunited.

'Go,' he says, peeling my arms from around his waist and making a shooing gesture with his hands.

I groan and pick up my bag.

'Okay then. I guess I'll see you on Sunday. Love you.'

'Love you too.'

I turn and walk out the door.

At the base of the apartment stairs, I'm greeting by a darkly tinted, shiny black sports car.

Jace gives the engine a little rev before getting out of the driver's side. He's dressed in a sharp black suit and wearing dark sunglasses, looking as though he's stepped out of a James Bond movie.

'Here, let me take your bags.'

'Thank you,' I say, handing my bag over to Jace, hoping that Matt isn't watching from the apartment window. It can't be easy for him to see me climb into a car with Jace, knowing he's going to be alone for the entire weekend.

Before I get into the car, I glance up at our apartment window and relax when I see that the curtains are still drawn, with not a twitch in sight. Matt has probably returned to his crossword puzzle. Either that or he's chatting to his online friends.

I put my seatbelt on and relish the comfort of the soft leather seats. The car smells like Jace, like the cologne he's always wearing, mixed with the new car scent.

'Let's go,' he says, and takes off, the engine rumbling and the speed pressing my back against the seat.

'So how did it go with your husband?' Jace asks, after we pull out of the car park.

'He was okay about it, actually.'

I glance out the window and watch the suburban houses whizz by. Suddenly having this new job and slowly putting money away isn't enough. I want that one hundred grand. And I want Matt booked in at the hospital for his operation as soon as possible.

'You've got that intense look on your face again,' says Jace, glancing at me briefly with raised brows before he directs his gaze back to the road.

'Oh I'm just thinking... about this weekend. Nervous, I guess. I've never sold a house before.'

Jace makes a sound in his throat and shakes his head. 'You're going to be a natural. I just know it.'

'Maybe,' I say, sitting up straighter in my seat. 'If you can give me a crash course before we do the home open, I'd appreciate it.' I glance at him quickly, hoping that I don't come across as too needy or demanding. 'Only if you have the time.'

'Of course. We can dial room service and eat dinner in my room tonight. I'll tell you everything you need to know.' He laughs when he sees the look on my face. 'Don't worry. You'll do great. I have a good feeling about this. In fact, I have a strong feeling that we'll be toasting with a bottle of expensive champagne by tomorrow night.'

I exhale and smile uneasily. 'Don't let me get my hopes up.'

He laughs again.

'You need to relax, Nadia. This house will sell. Sometimes we even get offers phoned in before the opening, without having to lift a finger. Trust me.'

'Okay. I trust you.'

'Good. I've booked us in for tomorrow night at the rooftop restaurant. The best table in the house. We're going to be celebrating your first sale at that dinner.'

'I hope so.'

Jace meets my gaze and smiles kindly before he directs his eyes back to the traffic. The freeway is already quite thick with cars.

'So much for beating the traffic,' he says, groaning.

But after half an hour of crawling, bumper to bumper, the highway finally opens up and Jace puts his foot down. In a matter of seconds the car is moving well over the speed limit. While the rumble of the engine exhilarates me, it also scares me.

Luckily Jace notices me gripping the grab handle above my window and eases his foot off the pedal until we are driving at a safer speed.

'Sorry. I've got a bit of a lead foot.' He grimaces. 'You'll need to remind me to slow down if I go too fast for you.'

'Don't worry, I will,' I say, my heart racing. 'I don't think we have much of a chance at selling this house if we're dead.'

'True that,' Jace says, grinning at me before he shifts his focus back to the road.

I exhale and try my best to relax against the seat and enjoy the journey.

Jace puts some music on, something modern and easy, and concentrates on the road, leaving me some time to think as I watch the houses thin out and the greenery increase as we pass through the more rural areas.

Jace seems so sure, so certain that we'll sell this property by the end of tomorrow.

Maybe I should finally allow myself to be hopeful.

I lean back against the head rest and close my eyes, picturing what life might be like for Matt and me if I get that commission.

No more repetitive rice and pasta dishes. We'll actually be able to afford some meat to eat. We might even be able to go out for a steak dinner every once in a while.

This money could really change our lives.

If Matt gets his operation, he'll be able eventually to return to work. And with both of us working, everything is going to change for the better.

And this time I allow myself to finally believe that it's possible.

8

We arrive at the hotel and pull into the valet parking driveway. After Jace removes our bags from the boot of the car, he hands his keys over to an immaculately dressed hotel employee. Two other staff members appear and take our luggage directly to our rooms.

While I wait for Jace check us in, I watch couples walking in and out, some on their own, and others with very young children not yet in school. I get carried away and picture Matt and I sometime in the future, on holiday with our own children.

'That's what I like to see. You're smiling,' Jace says, handing me a keycard. 'Stay in that positive mindset and we will definitely sell that property tomorrow. Rich men can't resist a beautiful smile.'

I quirk an eyebrow at him. 'What if a rich woman comes to view the property? And anyway, don't people get cancelled nowadays for telling someone they have a beautiful smile?'

He laughs. 'Well, if a rich woman shows up, then that's where I come in.'

I shake my head, but I'm smiling.

'They gave us adjoining rooms, so it'll make things easier for when we brainstorm.' He must have noticed my hesitation because he smiles. 'Don't worry. There's a lock on the adjoining door so when you get sick of hearing real estate jargon you can disappear into the safety of your room and lock the door.

His words set me at ease and, as we ride the glass elevator to the seventeenth floor, we are already discussing our plans for tomorrow.

'We'll rise early if you don't mind. Get to the property and give it a good once over. The client has already moved out, so a quick dusting of the benchtops, maybe a little bit of sweeping. And we'll open the windows to freshen the air and brighten the place up. I've brought along a diffuser and some candles – apple pie and cinnamon-scented.'

'I've heard about the scent thing. Someone once told me that they left a simmering stew on the stove top just to give a homely feel to their house when it was showing.'

'That is a good idea. But the scented candles are enough. This isn't exactly a house for your average family. Usually only couples are looking at this price or even singles. So homely isn't exactly what attracts my clientele.'

We exit the elevator and walk down a long corridor to our rooms.

'Here we are. Rooms 26 and 27. You can have 27. It's my lucky number.'

I smile. 'Thank you.'

Jace looks at his smart watch.

'How about you go freshen up and chill for a bit. I've got a bit of work to do so you're free for a couple of hours and then we can touch base before dinner, maybe around 5pm. Does that sound okay to you?'

He gestures towards the large window at the end of the corridor through which I can see the vivid blue of the Indian ocean. 'I highly recommend a walk on the beach. You'll love it.'

'Ooh, that sounds nice, actually.'

He disappears into his room and I tap the keycard to my door and enter my room where the soft scent of vanilla lingers in the air.

The room is stylishly furnished in dark grey and white, and the staff have left a bottle of bubbly on ice, and a tray of gourmet chocolates that look handmade, on the wooden desk.

They've left my travel bag at the foot of my bed and when I take a peek in the bathroom, I'm pleasantly surprised to find a spa bath in there.

But the best part of the room, hands down, is the ocean view.

It's stunning and when I step out onto the balcony, my head grows light and I grip the railing for support. I don't bother to peer down, as I'm afraid of heights, but I do plan on sitting out here later with a glass of bubbly to watch the sunset over the ocean. Hopefully our brainstorming session doesn't take all night. I'd like some free time to enjoy the luxury of a hotel room to myself.

My heart twinges with guilt when I think of Matt back home, stuck in the apartment in his special chair.

I take my phone out of my handbag and give him a call.

'Hey,' Matt says, answering on the second ring. 'Far out, he must have been speeding to have gotten you there so quickly.'

I detect a hint of bitterness, not just a hint, a lot. But if I put myself in his shoes and knew that he was spending a weekend away with an attractive woman who owned a fancy sports car, I'd probably feel the same.

'I thought I'd give you a call. I wish you were here.'

'So are you two sharing a room or what?'

'Of course not. I've got my own room. It's gorgeous. I'll take lots of photos.'

Matt's quiet on the other line.

'You got another package today. I opened it.'

My stomach tightens with dread. 'What was inside it?'

'A single red rose. A dead one.'

'Throw it out,' I say, my stomach turning.

'I've kept it. You need to take it to the police when you get back.'

'Maybe, but I know they're not going to do anything about a dead flower.'

My face heats up as I recall the embarrassment of showing the local police the contents of a parcel I was sent by my stalker a few months ago – a lingerie set. One of the officers joked to Matthew that maybe I was just trying to get out of trouble for spending too much money shopping online. It was mortifying and made me very angry that they weren't taking me seriously.

'Whatever,' he says, before sighing noisily into the phone.

'Are you okay, Matt? You were so positive about this only a few hours ago. Remember that I'm only doing it for us.'

'Yeah, I know. I just... I don't want to get my hopes up. I mean, we have so much riding on this. The operation, and the fact that we're going to be evict–'

'Going to be *what*?'

Matthew is quiet for a long time. My stomach drops.

'I know we've been behind on our rent, but we're not going to be evicted. They have to give us notice for that.

Matt sighs noisily again. 'I should have told you earlier but I didn't know how to say it.'

'What?'

'You know how we've been late on our rent?'

'Yeah.'

'Well, I don't want to put pressure on you, but we have to leave the apartment by the end of next week. The owner wants us out.'

'What? But we were only late twice over the past two months, and I've already paid this week's rent with my first pay. And they need to give us notice for this kind of thing. Six weeks I'm pretty sure.'

'That's what I need to tell you. Don't get mad. Promise me.'

I take a deep breath. 'I promise.'

'Someone came to the door and gave me an eviction notice six weeks ago. But I couldn't bring myself to tell you. You were already so stressed out about money, so I just screwed it up and threw it in the bin. I was drinking at the time and thought if I destroyed the letter, we could ignore it.'

'What on earth possessed you to do that? *Next week*?' I put my hand to my forehead and sit on the edge of the bed before my knees buckle beneath me.

'I'm sorry, Nards.'

'You should have told me, Matt.' I rake a hand through my hair. 'Where on earth are we going to live?'

'See how stressed you are? This is exactly why I didn't tell you.'

I bite down on all the angry words I want to say and instead focus my gaze on the glittering ocean view from my hotel window. I need to channel my emotions into something more productive than berating my husband. I need to use our dire situation as fuel, as motivation to sell this house. Because we are now officially one week away from living out of our car.

Something tinkers in the background.

'What's that sound?' I ask, but I don't need to ask, because I recognise it as ice clinking against glass.

'Don't get angry. There's a reason why I'm drinking. I also got a call from my nana's neighbour, George.'

'Oh no. Is she okay?'

'She's in hospital. She had a fall.'

'Oh I'm so sorry, Matt. Have you spoken to her?'

'Not yet. She's resting right now but they'll let me know when she's awake so I can call her.'

'Do you want me to go out and see her? I'm probably only an hour away.'

'No. No. You focus on that sale. I've... I've got a friend here that can drive me down.'

'But your back. Are you sure that's a good idea? The doctor said no long journeys.'

'She's my nana, Nards, and all I've got. What else am I supposed to do?'

'Yeah, I get it. I'm sorry. What a rotten time for me to be away.' I hear the tinkering of glass again and I can't help the fury I feel towards this so-called *friend* of Matt's. 'Who's your friend?'

'Oh, just a mate from my AA chat group. I'm alone right now, though. So we can talk properly.'

'Be careful please. Promise me you'll just have the one drink. And say a big hello to your nana when you see her.'

'I will. And Nards?'

'Yes?'

'You can do this. You'll make this sale. Then once I have the op and recover from it, I'll be able to work again and we can move away, escape that little creep stalker of yours. And you won't have to work for someone else anymore, you can stay home and do that cooking thing you've always wanted to do. We'll live somewhere safe, somewhere out in the country where nobody will find us. We can even start a family.'

'I hope so,' I say, my throat tightening with emotion. It all sounds like a dream, and so out of reach, but maybe my husband has enough belief for the both of us. 'I love you.'

'Love you too. See you on Sunday night.'

The hope in his voice should reassure me, but all it does is make me feel ill. What if the property doesn't sell. Then what?

'Yeah. See you then.'

9

At 5pm I get a knock on the adjoining door between our rooms. I unlock it and open the door to find Jace standing there dressed in a fresh pair of trousers and a pale green shirt that brings out the brown in his eyes.

'Are you ready to get brainstorming?' he asks, stepping aside to allow me into his room.

'Actually, could you give me five minutes? I was on the phone to Matthew and I haven't had a chance to change yet.'

Jace nods. 'Take all the time that you need. And don't knock, just let yourself in.

'Thanks.'

I close the door and quickly unpack my clothes. The conversation I had with Matt has completely derailed me and set me on edge. I spent the past hour staring into space and didn't even get a chance to go on that beach walk.

After choosing a pair of black jeans and a comfortable, beige button-up shirt, I take a quick shower then get dressed.

Around twenty minutes later, I enter Jace's room, knocking on the door beforehand despite Jace telling me that I didn't need to.

Jace, who's seated at the provided work desk, stands when he sees me.

The wooden desk is already covered with neat piles of paperwork as well as an opened laptop.

'Would you like a coffee?' he offers. 'I've just made one for myself.'

'Yes. Thank you. I'm feeling a little bit sleepy actually.'

Jace pops a pod into the machine and soon the scent of freshly brewed coffee that's already in the room intensifies.

He hands me a small white cup.

'Thanks,' I say, before taking a sip. It's heaven.

'Let's get straight to it,' says Jace, nodding towards a seat by the desk. I sit down and he remains standing.

'Now,' says Jace. 'This particular client, the owner of the property we are selling, has a huge portfolio. For him, selling this house doesn't change much for him. He is in no rush, there's no need for him to buy another property to move into because he already has multiple homes and apartments that he lives in and out of, not just in Australia, but across the globe.'

My heart sinks. If the owner of the property is in no rush to sell, he's not going to settle on the first offer he gets, he's going to want to choose the highest offer from multiple. And no matter what Jace says, I still find it difficult to imagine that there are a more than a few people out there who can afford to buy a ten-million-dollar property.

'But don't worry. Just because the owner isn't in a rush doesn't mean we can't speed things along a little.' He grins and claps his hands together. 'I don't do anything by halves, Nadia. We are going to get a buyer to make an offer at full price, maybe more, before the end of tomorrow.'

'But how can you be so sure?' I ask, cradling the coffee cup on my hands.

'Because I'm good at what I do. The owner of the property knows this too. That's why he trusts me.'

My heart rises a little.

'Okay. I'm going to have to take your word for it.'

'Good. But it doesn't mean we're going to be sitting around on our butts doing nothing. What we do this evening is what's most important. Tonight is about drumming up interest.'

'Okay.'

He sits on the edge of his bed and opens his laptop. 'Yesterday I sent an email out to my curated list of potential buyers, and already over twenty of them have replied asking for more information. Our job tonight is to call each of these potential buyers and give them all the information that they need and to also encourage them to attend the home open tomorrow. We don't want them making special, individual appointments. We're going to ask them all to show up at the same time, at twelve.'

'But wouldn't that mean we can't spend any one-on-one time with each client?'

Jace snaps his laptop shut. 'These men and women have big egos, Nadia. They can't handle anybody else winning the prize except themselves.'

'And the prize is the house. The latest hot property.'

'Bingo. Now. Let's work our way through this list. You can listen to me speak the first couple of times and then I'll hand it all over to you. Meanwhile I'll get you acquainted with the property using our 3D software so that by the time you arrive at the house tomorrow morning, you'll feel like you've been there before.'

'Okay. That all sounds doable.' My stomach flutters nervously. I don't like speaking on the phone with strangers, but I can hardly pike out. I need to show Jace that I'm serious about this job, and about this listing in particular. Even if it means faking confidence over the phone.

Jace smiles at me.

'Ready to get stuck in?' he asks.

I try to picture Matt and me living out of our car, the horrors of my husband trying to contort his already broken body into the small interior of the Pulsar.

No. That is not going to happen.

'Let's do this,' I say with conviction. Because there are no other options, other than to earn that commission this weekend.

10

It's after midnight by the time I return to the privacy of my own room, and I make sure to lock the adjoining door.

Working through the list of clients, speaking to each of them personally... it felt awkward at first. But once I got the hang of it, I genuinely felt as though I was building a rapport with our potential buyers. Which makes me feel a little more confident about the home open tomorrow.

Jace seemed impressed with my work. He kept giving me the big thumbs up every time I ended a call. Then afterwards we spent time poring over our notes and the necessary paperwork required for tomorrow until we could barely keep our eyes open.

Yawning, I spy the bottle of complimentary bubbly bobbing now, in a bucket of water instead of ice, but decide against it. I want to be bright-eyed and bushy-tailed for tomorrow's house viewing. I take the bottle out of the ice bucket and wipe it down with the provided white cloth and store it in the bar fridge.

Hopefully when tomorrow is over, and I return to my room, I can pop the bottle and celebrate the good news over the phone with Matthew.

I strip off and get into one of Matt's old T-shirts that I like to wear as a nightie and slip between the cool cotton sheets. They are a luxurious combination of a crisp yet satiny feel, and I spend half a minute sliding my arms and legs around under the covers just to enjoy it. I haven't slept a night without Matthew since before we were married and it feels strange having so much room in the bed.

Lonely too.

Sleep doesn't come easily, and the more that I try to force myself to sleep, the more awake and alert I become. Eventually, at around 3am, my lids flutter closed and I drift into a light and fitful sleep.

I'm woken, after what seems like only ten minutes, by a knock at the adjoining door and I stumble out of bed and groggily unlock and open it to find Jace dressed in a navy suit, a crisp white shirt and a tie.

'You're up already?'

'It's eight o'clock, Nadia,' he says, a puzzled look on his face. 'Remember we agreed to go down to breakfast together before the home open to go over our list.'

I glance at my phone and see it flashing silently. I must have been sleeping so deeply to have slept through the vibrations.

'I'm so sorry,' I say, putting hand to my forehead. 'I was awake for most of the night. I feel awful. You must think I'm so unprofessional.'

'No. Don't worry about it. How about I go downstairs and get us a table and you can come when you're ready. Home open isn't until noon so we have plenty of time.'

'Okay. Thanks.'

His eyes travel down my T-shirt and rest on my long bare legs and he blinks and puts his sunglasses on. 'Okay, so I'll leave you to it and meet you downstairs.'

'I won't be long,' I say.

Now I wished that I'd washed my hair last night as I don't have the time to blow dry it this morning. I give it a generous spray of dry shampoo after a quick shower and then put my makeup on and get dressed.

I'm downstairs twenty minutes later and find Jace on the phone sitting at a corner table overlooking the sea.

It's a breathtaking view and I allow myself to imagine Matt and I coming here for a nice holiday after he recovers from his back surgery. We could sit here and indulge in delicious, lazy breakfasts while we make plans for our future.

Jace puts away his phone and glances at his Rolex when I sit down.

'Wow. My wife would have taken at least an hour.' He whistles. 'You were less than half an hour. I'm impressed.'

'I may have rushed things a little,' I say, hoping my hair doesn't look too oily.

Jace smiles. 'You look lovely.' His face turns serious. 'But can I suggest something? And promise you won't get offended?'

'Wash my hair? It's too oily, isn't it? I knew I should have washed it.'

'No,' he says, laughing, his eyes locking with mine. 'Your hair, your face... everything is beautiful. You're perfect.'

It's almost an ordeal to have his eyes fixed so intently on me right now. My heart is racing, my cheeks feel hot, my palms are sweaty.... I try to imagine how his wife must feel being gazed at like this all the time. She and Jace must spend all their downtime in the bedroom if this is the way he looks at her all the time.

I clear my throat and try to remain focused and professional.

'Then what is your suggestion?' I ask.

Jace inhales deeply through his nose, then exhales, his eyes on mine the entire time.

'We need to look the part. And I understand that this is last minute so you wouldn't have had time to prepare or go out and purchase anything, and I apologise for that. But would you, as an apology from me for not giving you much notice, allow me to take you shopping for an outfit for today? I know a nice little boutique that my wife adores. I'd say about eighty percent of her wardrobe is from this place. I reckon we could fit you out in something that would help you to feel more confident today.'

‘Oh, okay.’ I look down at my cheap skirt and mended shirt I’m wearing. Even though the mended part is hidden by the collar, Jace must have noticed.

‘I’m sorry. I haven’t been able to buy any new work clothes yet.’

I end up telling him about the eviction notice that Matthew kept from me.

‘He kept it from you? Why on earth would he do that?’

‘To save me from the stress.’ I shrug. ‘In his roundabout way, he was looking out for me.’

‘No offense, but your husband is...’ Jace pauses and looks at me. ‘He’s an idiot. Sorry. But it needs to be said.’

‘He’s just trying to protect me. He’s having a really hard time right now and he does these kinds of things to save me from getting upset. That’s all it is. He just can’t stand to see me hurt.’

Jace shrugs. ‘We all need to learn how to deal with our feelings. Getting hurt is what makes us stronger and more resilient. He’s not protecting you, he’s hindering you.’

‘When you put it that way, then yes. But I know that’s not his intention.’

‘Okay then,’ Jace says, ending the subject. ‘How about we eat breakfast, run through our client list again, then head out to the boutique and get you kitted out.’

‘Okay. But you need to let me pay you back when I get paid next week.’

‘You mean the pay fattened significantly with the commission?’ he says, grinning.

I laugh at first and then frown.

‘But won’t it take weeks until the sale goes through and you receive the funds?’

He shrugs. ‘Usually, of course. But we’re talking people who have millions sitting in their bank accounts. They don’t have to visit their banks for approval, they can make cash offers and boom, the house is not only under offer, its technically sold then and there. Well, at least until the paperwork is drawn up and signed and the funds are transferred.

'That's crazy.'

'It is. It's a mad world out there. But an interesting one. And the best part is, there's enough money to go around for everyone. If you want it enough.' He turns serious again and fixes his intense gaze on me. 'Do you want it enough, Nadia?'

I nod, my stomach fluttering anxiously. There's too much riding on this.

'Yes. Of course I want it enough. One hundred percent.'

Jace relaxes back against his seat and nods.

'That's what I like to hear.' He drums the tabletop with his fingertips. 'Now, let's order breakfast. I'm starving.'

11

After breakfast, Jace drives me to the boutique he was talking about.

My stomach flutters when we enter the store and for a second I feel like Julia Roberts in *Pretty Woman*. It's the kind of place that's too expensive even for window shopping. It smells expensive too, like entering a room filled with gardenias and jasmine.

Jace introduces me to an auburn-haired, middle-aged sales woman at the counter and asks her to help me to pick out 'several outfits, for business *and* pleasure' and to put them all on his account. For a horrifying second, I wonder if he's going to want me to try them all on for him, but then he pulls out his phone to take a call and indicates, through hand gestures and soundless mouthing, that he'll return in thirty minutes to collect me, before he disappears out of the boutique.

I'm not sure where to begin, and feel a little panicked that I need to pick 'several' outfits within thirty minutes, but thankfully Marta is a great help and twenty-five minutes later, I'm waiting out the front of the store, carrying a white branded shopping bag. I ended up choosing a long black tube skirt that is so soft against my skin it feels luxurious to wear, and a navy pant suit, a cream skirt suit, as well as a demure but pretty evening dress – for that all important celebratory dinner at the rooftop restaurant tonight.

When Jace pulls up and gets out to take my bag and open my car door, I feel slightly uncomfortable.

Although I'm extremely happy with my outfits, it doesn't feel right that a man that I've only known for a little under two weeks has paid for them.

'I'll pay you back for these,' I say, as I slide into the leather passenger seat. 'Gradually, of course.'

He grins down at me and shuts my car door. When he gets into the driver's seat he's still grinning.

'I'll just take it out of the enormous commission you'll be earning from today's sale.' He taps his temple. 'We need to think positive, behave assured as though the sale has already happened.'

I grin and shrug. 'I chose a dress for the celebratory dinner tonight.'

'Brilliant. You're doing it already then. That's the law of attraction,' he says. 'And you'll see it in action today.'

'I'm sure I will,' I say, hoping that just by saying it, I'm willing it into effect.

I don't tell him that for the past six months I've already been trying my best to attract more money into my life. I discovered affirmations on the internet one day after googling '888 number' because at the time I was seeing those three digits everywhere – on two vehicle number plates, an address, and a phone number. Apparently seeing a repetition of numbers is the way our guardian angels... or the universe, tries to communicate with us.

'My life is filled with wealth and my prosperity is limitless' is what the website I stumbled upon advised me to affirm.

I've been chanting these words in the shower almost daily for the past six months but so far it has yielded nothing. In fact our finances have gotten worse as time has progressed. Although, to be fair, here I am with a large glossy white bag filled with expensive clothes while being driven around in a flashy sports car. Perhaps the law of attraction exists after all.

'Okay, let's go straight to the property,' Jace says, once we're buckled into our seats.

‘I thought I was going to go back to the hotel room to change into one of these outfits.’

‘No time,’ Jace says, his eyes on the road as he floors the accelerator. ‘But don’t worry. This house is huge. You can get dressed in one of the twelve bedrooms.’

‘Oh, okay.’ I would have liked to have been able to redo my hair and makeup to match my new outfit but I guess my neat low bun and minimal makeup will have to do.

‘Don’t worry,’ says Jace, as though reading my mind. ‘You’ll look fantastic and you’ll do great. Just be yourself. Welcome the guests like we said. Did you memorise the list?’

‘I did.’ I straighten my back and clear my throat. ‘I look forward to asking Mr Johnson if he enjoyed his recent trip to New Zealand with his dog Inky Winky.’

Jace laughs. ‘Trust me. He’ll love it. Our clients love to be coddled. If we make them feel special, then they’ll start to believe they are special enough to deserve a ten-million-dollar home.’

‘It makes sense.’ Before I can stop myself, I tap my temple, just like Jace has a habit of doing, then cringe into my seat when he notices.

‘It’s called mirroring,’ he says, as he changes lanes then turns onto another street. ‘You’re subconsciously building rapport and establishing a connection with me. This is exactly what we’ll be doing today with our clients.’

We’ve left town and are now driving along the coast beside a long stretch of beachfront homes. The ocean looks glorious, its surface like glass.

‘Okay,’ he says, ‘here we are.’

Jace’s car slows down and we pull into a large, paved double driveway of a gorgeous four-storey resort-style home.

‘Wow.’ I take a moment to drink in the gleaming white walls, the large tinted windows. Then there’s the stone statues flanking the entrance and the water fountain in the garden... this home is stunning.

‘It’s pretty impressive, isn’t it?’ says Jace.

He parks the car and we both get out.

The salty sea breeze tickles an escaped tendril of my hair and tugs at my clothes. I inhale deeply. I've always dreamed of living by the sea. If I lived at this house, I'd never leave.

Jace retrieves a black designer sports bag from the boot of his car, while I carry my shopping bag.

'See these gardens?' Jace points out the immaculate front garden. The freshly cut lawn with sharp edges, and the carefully pruned shrubs. There's not a single weed in sight. 'Even though the owner only visits twice a year, he hires a gardener to come each week.'

'Wow,' I say again. 'It does look amazing, though, so it's worth it. If you have that kind of money, of course.'

Jace takes out his keys and opens the front door. We step inside.

'Okay,' he says, 'first thing, lets open all the curtains and windows and let that fresh sea air into the home. After that we'll light the scented candles and then you can go upstairs and get dressed while I do a quick once over on the surfaces with the duster.'

'Sounds good,' I say, setting my handbag and boutique bag on the dining room table.

We work quickly and efficiently. It's a big job because the house is so huge, but thirty minutes later, we've got the windows and curtains open, all surfaces have been dusted, floors swept, and the house is bright, airy and filled with the tantalising scent of the candles.

'I'm going to get dressed,' I say, taking the bag with me as I head up the elegant marble staircase.

'Wait a moment,' Jace says from the bottom of the stairs. He motions for me to come back down. I do.

'Let me take a look.'

I hand him the bag and after inspecting all the outfits, he chooses the cream suit. The skirt is a bit on the short side but Marta kept telling me that it fit me like a glove so I just had to get it. 'This. Wear this.'

I take the clothes and head upstairs, mildly disturbed that I'm wearing something that he chose. But he's the experienced one here, so I guess he knows what works for home opens.

Five minutes later I'm dressed and tugging on the skirt self-consciously as I come down stairs.

Jace must hear the clack of my heels as I find him waiting, watching my descent, his dark brown eyes widening slightly.

'You look *amazing*,' he says, his brows raised. 'Like... Wow.' Then he slaps his hands together and his face grows serious. 'Okay. We're ready to go. I've popped the signs out and moved my car so that there's ample parking and all we have to do now is wait for our clients to arrive.'

My stomach flutters with anxiety.

'Oh God, I feel sick,' I mutter, wringing my hands together.

'Don't worry. You'll do amazing. You'll *be* amazing. Trust me. Just make these men and women feel like a million dollars, like they deserve this property.'

'Will do,' I say with a serious nod.

'And I'll be right by your side,' he says, stepping a little closer and offering me a smile of reassurance.

My heart flutters in response. Jace is devastatingly attractive when he smiles. And the intoxicating scent of his aftershave doesn't help. But apart from my annoying biological responses to his attractiveness, I have zero interest in him in that way. All I want to do is get this sale over with and return to Matt with the news that he can get the operation done.

Somebody knocks on the stained-glass window panel beside the front door, the shadow behind the coloured glass is tall and wide-set.

'Go on, you greet them,' Jace says, waving me towards the front door. 'You can do this.'

I nod. And after sucking in a deep breath and slowly exhaling, I put on my brightest smile and open the screen door.

'Joseph Stark,' the man says, beaming back at me. 'You must be new.'

‘Nadia Freeman.’ I offer him my hand and he shakes it. ‘Welcome to number eight, Seaview Lane.’

Jace takes a step back and gives me an encouraging nod, so I continue.

‘Let me take you through,’ I say. ‘How is your wife doing after her knee surgery?’

Joseph Stark nods and smiles. ‘She’s doing fantastic. But she’ll be a lot happier if I secure this property.’

My stomach flutters with excitement and I glance over my shoulder at Jace who gives me a discreet thumbs-up and I grin at him before turning back to Joseph Stark.

It takes a good fifteen minutes for me to show Joseph through each room in the home as well as the backyard, the indoor swimming pool, and the four double garages – insulated and weatherproofed to prevent any damaging sea salt and moisture from entering, which makes them perfect for housing the vintage cars he collects.

‘Sold,’ Joseph says, slapping his hands together in a loud, echoing clap.

For a second, I stand there, staring at him, my mouth slightly open in shock.

He laughs. ‘I know what I want when I see it.’

I release a shaky laugh and relax my shoulders. This is really happening. I can’t believe it. But it’s actually happening. I’m going to be earning my first commission.

We take a seat at the dining table to talk figures. I can see that Jace has laid everything out for me. Each set of forms in their correct order.

I take the first one, which Jace has handily pre-filled.

‘Okay, so we have your details already. Let’s move straight to the offer.’

‘Add a hundred grand to the price,’ Joseph says. He looks at Jace. ‘This is exclusively for this lovely young lady. A separate commission just for her.’

My fingers quiver and I drop my pen, but thankfully Jace bends to pick it up and comes to sit at the table, right beside me. His calm presence soothes my frazzled nerves, and I start to breathe a little easier.

'Let's get this show on the road,' Joseph says. 'I need to go buy my wife some flowers and surprise her with the good news.'

12

The view from the rooftop bar is as stunning as Jace had promised. He managed to get us the best table with the most stunning views of the glittering Indian ocean which right now is tinted gold with the setting sun.

'Did you tell Matthew?' Jace asks, as we tap our flutes of proper French champagne.

A pleasantly warm, salty breeze tickles the lock of hair that I've allowed to escape my up-do. I'm wearing the dress that I got this morning from the boutique and I feel like a million dollars sitting up here with Jace. But I also feel awful for Matt, sitting at home alone. Even if he did sound ecstatic over the phone about the sale and, uncharacteristically, practically ordered me to go out and celebrate, to enjoy myself, I can't help but feel guilty that he's missing out on this.

'Yes. I wasn't going to, as I didn't want to get his hopes up in case something goes wrong. But... my excitement couldn't be contained. I think I lasted about two seconds before I spilled.'

Jace chuckles. 'Nothing will go wrong. And anyway, we still have the other buyers on file if Joseph flakes, which he won't.'

'Why didn't the others show?' I ask, twirling my glass in my hand. 'We had twelve confirmed clients to view the house.' I grin, the champagne already warming the blood in my veins. 'I'm a little disappointed that I missed out on asking Mr Johnson about Inky Winky.'

Jace laughs.

Although I'm smiling, the lack of clients has been bothering me all afternoon. I kept expecting other buyers to walk in while we were seated with Joseph but they didn't.

'Actually, I should have told you. While you were showing Joseph around, I called them all to tell them the property was gone. Only because I know what Joseph is like. Once he sees what he likes he always offers more than the asking price. It's just the way he likes to do things.' Jace winks. 'And don't worry, He's loaded to the hilt. This is just a minor chink in the amour of his wealth.'

I nod slowly and take another sip of the champagne. Ten million dollars described as a minor chink is something I thought I'd never hear in my lifetime but here we are.

'And I'm going to honour my promise as well as Joseph's. You'll get half of my commission as well as Joseph's extra one hundred thousand.'

'Wait... what?' I pinch myself on my thigh under the table, because I must be dreaming.

'Which would double your earnings to–'

'Two hundred thousand dollars. I can't believe it,' I say, shaking my head.

Jace meets my gaze, his eyes dark and serious. 'You earned every cent of it. So don't go feeling like it's charity, because it's not. When we deal with our higher end customers, this is the kind of money they throw around.'

'Wow.' I shake my head. 'How the other half live,' I say, then I whistle and take a long sip of my champagne, emptying the flute. 'Oops.'

Jace tops me up quickly and soon another bottle appears.

Two more glasses and some tapas plates later, I'm feeling a bit tipsy so I excuse myself to go the bathroom.

Once I'm at the basin, I splash cold water onto the back of my neck with a paper towel and try to straighten up a little. I drank way too fast, mostly because I was in shock, and am still in shock, that I've doubled my earnings. But I need to stay professional. 'Only water from now on,' I tell myself aloud as I stare myself in the mirror.

My phone buzzes in my handbag and I take it out to find a message from Matthew.

He's made an online appointment to see his GP to get the operation booked. I write back telling him how happy I am for him. He sends back a lot of celebratory emojis.

Then he sends me a whole bunch of links to properties down south, as though he's had them on standby all day. He's excited, I can tell. This money has brought new life to my husband already. I can't wait to see him tomorrow, and I text him exactly that. He responds immediately with another flood of celebratory emojis.

To think we have the money to pay for somewhere to live instead of being turned out onto the street next week! Thank God for this sale and thank God for Joseph Stark.

My phone buzzes again. It's Matt again.

> *I love you so much, Nadia, and I can't thank you enough for putting up with my crap the past few months. This operation is going to change our lives and I promise you I'm never touching alcohol again. All I care about now is giving you the best life possible, the dream life you deserve.*
> *Love you xx*

I respond by telling him how much I love him, followed by several heart emojis, then I put my phone away, grinning as I walk back to the table.

But when I return, Jace has his phone to his ear and is engaged in a heated conversation out on the balcony by the bar. The background music is fairly loud so I can't hear a word of what he's saying, but judging by the wild gestures and jerky hand movements, I can tell that it's not good news.

My heart takes a dramatic dive into the pit of my stomach. Even if we do have a list of clients to turn to, lighting isn't going to strike twice. I'm not going to be getting any more bonuses of the Joseph Stark variety.

Still feeling a little dizzy, I pour myself a glass of water and sip it while I wait until Jace finishes his conversation and returns to the table. He looks completely harassed. His hair is mussed up and his cheeks are flamed with anger.

'Is everything okay?' I ask, even though it's clear that everything is not okay.

'He's not going through with it. He's found a fault in the home. He came back to view it again this evening and the next-door neighbour came out and introduced himself and told him that part of the property's yard is actually the neighbour's property, so the man said that he technically has rights to access Joseph's backyard and make use of the side gate for easy access to the beach.' He pauses and drains his flute and pours himself another. 'Anyway, unfortunately, Joseph wants out. He said he doesn't like sharing his things.'

'What about the other clients? You said we could turn to the list if Joseph pulls out of the deal.'

'Apparently the neighbour, who sounds like a grumpy old bastard, told Joseph that he plans on informing anyone who comes to view the property in the future.' Jace sighs. 'These buyers, Nadia, they all move in the same circle. The property is temporarily screwed and unsellable until we sort this out. If it can be sorted that is. The whole point to the private gate to the beach is that it's private. People like that kind of exclusivity.'

'But can't the neighbour use his own gate?'

'Apparently, he hasn't got one. His back wall is too high or some rubbish. It's easier for him to use the next-door property.'

Reality crashes down on me, like an icy wave.

I won't be getting my commission.

Matt won't be getting the operation.

My phone vibrates in my bag, which is resting on my lap and I take it out and see more links for country homes for sale that Matt has sent me.

My stomach churns sickly.

'There is one thing Joseph Stark did offer.' Jace shakes his head angrily. 'A way for you to still get your money.' He meets my gaze. 'I hope you don't mind, but I told him about your predicament.' Jace sighs. 'So anyway, he made me an offer. A proposal. A sick one at that.' Jace takes a long sip of his champagne. 'But I told him to go to hell.'

'What's the proposal?'

Jace shakes his head. 'You wouldn't want to know. Trust me. And anyway, I can't tell you here in front of these people.'

'The music's loud. Nobody will hear you,' I say, prodding Jace to tell me.

'No. Not here. We need to head out to the property where it's completely private. I'll tell you there.' Jace looks me in the eye, his dark eyes intense. 'It's wild though. As I said, I told him to go to hell. But I guess I owe it to you to tell you what he proposed.'

'We're going there now? But we've had too much to drink. You can't drive.'

'I'll order an Uber.' He gets his phone out and taps on it several times. 'Done. Come on.' He settles the bill, buys another bottle of champagne to go and he takes me by the hand and leads me to the elevator.

We get into the Uber car, wordlessly, and once we're dropped off at the property, Jace gets the keys out and opens the empty house.

'Why did you have the keys on you tonight?'

Jace shrugs. 'I don't know. I forgot to put them away.'

'Okay.' My brain feels fuzzy, but the chilly sea air is helping with the dizziness I was feeling earlier.

Jace brings two glasses down from the high cupboards in the kitchen and leads me into the living room where he turns on a lamp and sets the glasses on the coffee table.

'Okay,' he says, after handing me my drink. 'This is the part where I tell you what Joseph Stark has in mind for the two of us.'

13

I sit back, my glass empty now, my head even lighter than before.

'So you're telling me that Joseph Stark owns an online sex website. A porn platform?'

'Yes.'

'And he wants us to have sex, and film it for him, for his kinky clients' perverted pleasure?'

'Apparently there are people out there who have a kink for nailing real estate agents inside empty homes.' Jace shrugs. 'I don't get it either.'

'So you knew this about him and said nothing to me?' I rub the bare skin of my arms as I tremble at the sudden drop in temperature, and the pure horror of what Joseph Stark has proposed. 'He seemed like such a nice guy. Unbelievable.'

'With all due respect, just because he runs a fantasy sex site doesn't mean he's a bad guy. He donates to charities and helps the homeless. There is a need for his business. There are lonely men and women all over the world who take comfort from the fact that they can log onto to his secured site and have their needs met. It helps to replace the lack of intimacy in their life. Not everyone is lucky enough to have found their partners like you or me.'

'But you said you told him to go to hell.'

'I did... but I started thinking in the car ride over. Maybe it's the drink talking, but I know how much you need this money, and now I don't know how long we're going to be tied up with this property issue. So...' He pauses and opens his palms. 'Maybe we should consider it.'

'Consider it?' I get up and start pacing the living room. 'You actually think this is okay? Two married people being filmed having sex with each other? A boss and his employee.'

I head for the door. 'I need to go home. I'm going to get an Uber back to the hotel and then I'll...' I stop when I realise that I can't afford an Uber from this house back to the hotel, let alone all the way home.

Tears prickle my eyes as I think about Matt and I being turfed out of our home next week. I picture the disappointment in Matt's eyes when I return home tomorrow to tell him that I didn't get the money.

'I'm sorry, Nadia. I hate that you're in this predicament. But...' He shakes his head. 'I can't believe I'm saying this, but I'm actually happy to go through with it if you are.'

'It's the alcohol talking,' I tell him.

But Jace shakes his head. 'It's not. I want to help you.'

I sit back down on the couch and decline the offer of a fresh glass of bubbly. If I do this, I need to be thinking as straight as possible which is difficult given how much we've already had to drink.

'What about our faces? I can't be seen on a website like that. What if Matt stumbles onto it, or if one of his friends sees it and sends him the link. I couldn't live with myself if Matt found out. He'd leave me. I know he would. My marriage would be over in an instant.'

Jace meets my eye. 'Look. We don't have to do this, and to tell you the truth, I don't really want to. But I want to help you out of your situation, help solve your financial problems.'

'I can't betray Matt. I just can't.'

'But what will you do next week when you get evicted from your apartment? Your husband's back won't last sleeping inside your small car. I mean, I could probably front up a week's worth of motel stays for you both, and try to fob it off as a work expense, but that's about all I can do.'

I shake my head. 'We won't be able to find a new place in a week, even with my new job. And with the current housing crisis and mile-long tenant waiting lists, we're well and truly screwed.' I wipe the tears from my eyes and stare up at the ceiling, hating myself for what I'm about to say.

'Call Joseph Stark, or message him... whatever. Tell him I'll do it.'

'Are you sure?'

I nod. 'But I don't want to show my face.' I think back to when I was bringing Joseph through the twelve rooms. 'There's a wardrobe in one of the upstairs bedrooms with clothes still in it. There were masquerade masks hanging up on a wall hook. If we can wear those, then yes, I'll do it.'

Inside my head a more sensible voice is screaming at me not to do this, that I'm crazy. But I shut her out.

Jace sends a message on his phone and it almost immediately pings back.

He's agreed to the masks.

I shudder to think of Joseph, sitting in a dark, luxurious basement somewhere, his face grey in the light of a computer screen as he waits for a video of me and Jace having sex to upload.

'When will we get the money?' I ask Jace, feeling bolder now. I'm the one who is calling the shots, and that at least makes this situation a little more bearable.

'Probably next week.'

'Tell him I want it by Monday. Two hundred thousand dollars.'

'He only offered the one hundred thousand. The money he was going to give *you* extra. Not your half of the commission as well.'

'Well I want it all,' I say. 'Tell him I want two hundred thousand. And that's just for me. You can negotiate your own money.'

Jace pales a little and he stares at me like he's just created a monster.

'Excuse me for a minute,' he says, tapping his phone and then putting it to his ear. 'Maybe you can go upstairs and find the masks.'

Jace disappears into the kitchen and I hear him talking to Joseph as I head upstairs to the third-floor master bedroom. Inside the wardrobe I find the masks and choose two glittery gold ones. They'll go well with my dress and Jace's tie.

When I come downstairs and find Jace in the kitchen, he looks grim and my stomach churns nervously. Maybe I've pushed Joseph Stark too hard with my demands. He might have revoked the proposition.

'He's agreed. You'll be getting two hundred thousand dollars in your bank account by Monday. Bearing in mind, it may take a few days for your bank to process it.'

'Good. So why do you look so worried? You're making me nervous.'

'I'm about to cheat on my wife, Nadia. That's why.' He swears and turns, leaning against the counter. 'I don't know if I can do it.'

Alarm makes my heart beat faster. I can't believe that I'm actually fearful that Jace will back out of this... of us *sleeping* together for a *sex video*. But I can't lose that money. I just can't. Not now that I've already promised Matt the moon.

I take out my phone and see that Matt has sent another message with more hearts as well as little money bags emojis.

> *I'm so proud of you, Nads. Honestly. When did I get so lucky. Can't believe I'm going to finally get this op done... to sit in a proper chair, and to have sex again, lol. Can't wait to treat you right. You've given me life again. Love you xx*

I stow my phone away in my handbag and set it on the counter.

'We need to think of this as a business transaction, Jace. There's no heart in it. It's just business. We perform our duties, and with these masks on, hopefully we can pretend we're someone else while we do it.'

He turns and takes the mask I offer him. 'And once we're done, we take these masks off, strip ourselves of these identities, then lock up the house.' I offer an encouraging smile. 'We can drive away and forget it ever happened.'

'I hope I can forget,' Jace says, holding my gaze, his eyes as dark as the ocean outside the kitchen window.

'Okay, so where should we do this?' I ask, impatient to get it over with.

Jace sighs and rubs at his forehead. He looks miserable.

'Joseph wants to film us on the kitchen bench. That's the fantasy apparently. I'm a potential buyer and you're the agent, doing your best to convince me to hand over my money.'

I nod, swallowing down the nausea rising up in my throat.

'Okay. Do we just film it on our phones then?'

'Yeah. I'll use mine.'

My skin prickles at the idea of there being footage of me at the mercy of Jace. But I think of the money and of Matt, excitedly scrolling through his phone looking for potential houses to start our new life in.

'Okay. But you need to promise me that once you've sent it off to Joseph, that you delete it from your phone. I'll need to watch you.'

'Of course. I don't want my wife finding it. She knows my password and borrows my phone all the time. Maybe to check for suspect messages, I don't know. But I'm definitely not keeping this on my phone.'

I nod. 'Okay, good. Now let's do this before I chicken out.'

Jace agrees and sets up his phone on the other side of the kitchen, his hands trembling, and makes sure that the frame captures the full view of us on the bench.

'Don't worry, with these masks on, nobody will know who we are,' I say.

Jace nods at my words of encouragement as we position ourselves against the kitchen bench.

His hand still trembles as he reaches up to lightly caresses my cheek, a move so intimate, it catches my breath and makes my heart pound.

Then he bends his head and presses his warm lips to my neck. I groan as a wave of desire floods my veins.

But although my body is responding to Jace's kisses and his touch, my mind is on Matt.

14

I blink at the harsh sunlight streaming in through the curtains, which I'd left wide open yesterday afternoon and forgot to close last night when we arrived, very late, at our hotel rooms.

My stomach churns sickly as I recall what I'd done last night with Jace. A secret that will haunt us both forever, threatening to poison our marriages if we let it.

After we'd completed the deed, and Jace had sent the video then promptly deleted it from his phone, I told him that I was going to quit working for him as soon as the money hit my account. He nodded in understanding and didn't even try to talk me out of it. He looked about as uncomfortable as I felt.

The only way I'm going to be able to remotely forget last night is if I never see Jace again. When he drops me off at my apartment this afternoon, it'll be the last time I see him.

A shiver takes hold and I tug the doona up to my chin. Although I'm trying my best to block out what we did last night, it's next to impossible.

The phone rings, startling me, and when I see that it's Matt, I can't bear to answer it. Last night he kept sending me messages, and all I could do was respond with smiling emojis, pretending that I am just as excited and happy as he is about the money. But it's going to be a lot harder to fake it over the phone, and harder still to his face.

I get a message from Jace.

Be ready in the foyer by 9am.

I send him a thumbs up then drag myself out of bed.

My head thumps and my mouth is dry. I don't think I'll ever be able to drink champagne again without thinking of Jace's lips trailing down my neck, and our bodies moving together against the cold marble kitchen bench of 8 Seaview Lane.

I shake the image out of my head and go into the bathroom to take a cold shower. The water is ice cold but I manage to stay under it long enough to wash my hair and scrub my body. Although I'd already showered Jace away from my body last night when I got back to my room, I feel the need to do it again today.

When my skin is pink and raw, I step out of the shower and dry off, trying my best to concentrate on Matt. On the huge smile he'll be wearing when I see him in a few hours' time.

That's what will make all of this worth it. The fact that Matt will be able to finally get his operation and reclaim his life.

Feeling slightly better, I get dressed, dry and style my hair then put on some light makeup. After I've packed all my things, I realise that I'm ready a little earlier than expected. So I boil the little hotel kettle and make myself a cup of tea.

After I've drunk that, I realise it's time.

Jace is already waiting for me in the foyer and when we lock eyes, he quickly looks away. He's as embarrassed as I am, which oddly makes me feel a little better. I'm not the only monster in this situation. We're both just as bad as each other for accepting Joseph's Stark's proposition.

When the valet parks the car in front of us, Jace takes my bag and puts it in the boot and then opens the passenger door for me.

'Thanks,' I barely whisper. I slide into the seat and buckle myself in.

The ride home is quiet, as expected, and heavy with the weight of our consciences.

When we finally arrive at my apartment block, I could almost cry I'm so relieved to be home.

'Thank you,' I say, glancing at him quickly. Jace holds my gaze, his eyes filled with pain, and for a moment I'm breathless.

'I'm so sorry it turned out like this, Nadia. I wanted you to get your money, but I wish we didn't–'

'Don't say it. Please. I feel bad enough as it is. I'm going to have to go in and face my husband now, and put on a happy face. Don't make me feel any worse than I already do.'

Jace blinks. 'Of course.' He nods. 'You two won't be in danger of having to live on the streets anymore. And your husband will get his operation.' Jace forces a smile. 'I'm being selfish. You should go in there with a big smile because you actually deserve it.'

'Thanks,' I say, knowing how difficult it is for Jace to be faking his joy. 'I guess this is goodbye.'

He nods. 'I'll make sure you get the money. I'll do something to make it all legit. Don't worry about a thing.'

'Thank you.' I step out of the car.

Jace pops the boot and gets out to hand me my travel bag and the boutique bag filled with the new clothes he purchased for me.

'Goodbye, Nadia.'

'Goodbye.'

He gets into the car and speeds out of the car park. Once he's around the corner and his sleek black vehicle is out of sight, I breathe a sigh of welcome relief.

'You can do this,' I mutter to myself as I make my way up the stairs. 'You sold that property... you did, until the problem with the neighbour came up. But you did actually sell it, so it's technically not a lie. You earnt that money. And you're going to go in there and give Matthew the biggest reason to smile. Two hundred thousand reasons.'

I smile. Because I am happy about the money, about what it can bring us.

The apartment door opens and Matt stands there grinning at me.

I let out a squeal and laugh, which is easy and not a lie. I've never been so happy to see my husband in my entire life.

I wrap my arms around his waist – careful not to squeeze him too tightly.

And vow to never let go.

15

Six months later

I'd never thought I'd say that I like living in the country. We've only been here for just over a month, so of course it's early days, but so far I love it.

Our property, which had originally belonged to Matt's grandmother, is located inland, about fifteen minutes away from a nearby coastal town called Saltbush Bay. The land is bordered by a thick forest, which feels, at times, like I'm being protected by nature's own fortress. The serenity and the solitude out here helps me to forget and allows me to pretend that our former life was nothing but a bad dream.

But on the other hand, the forest can make me feel isolated and vulnerable. If my stalker were to learn that we'd moved out here, I'm not sure that I'd feel so safe.

Matt's nan passed away just after he'd had his operation. She'd had another fall, this time while out for a walk in the forest. She was found in a weak condition the next morning by her neighbour, George, her pulse barely there. She sadly died before the ambulance reached her.

Matt blamed himself, and, as a result, spent the first few weeks of his recovery at our temporary caravan park accommodation feeling overwhelmed with guilt for not having been there to support her. I'd offered plenty of times to drive down myself and check on her, but Matt had waved away my offer because he knew that his grandmother wasn't keen on me and he didn't want to upset her.

I would have loved to have been able to form a bond with her, if she'd allowed me the chance to. Not having any family of my own, it would have been nice. But she didn't want that and I respected her right to choose. It does make me feel a little sad whenever I look out at the forest, like I am now from the kitchen window, a steaming mug of coffee in hand, to know that she died out there all alone.

I shiver. It also creeps me out to know that she died on the property. When Matt first suggested we move out here into his grandmother's house – which he inherited once she passed – I begged him to sell it instead, so that we could choose a place together. But he wouldn't have it and because he was grieving at the time, I let it slide. It's a huge sacrifice on my part, because I really didn't want to move into a house that was owned by someone who resented me. But I wasn't exactly in a position to be making demands after what I did in Busselton. So here we are.

As soon as the money was transferred into my account, I put in a leave notice, which Jace allowed me to act on immediately instead of working for two more weeks more as per the contract I'd signed. Which I was grateful for. But I suppose he didn't exactly want to see my face every day either. I also dropped the expensive clothes that he purchased for me at a charity store.

Most importantly, I have been doing my best to rid myself of the memory, spending countless nights replaying the weekend at Busselton inside my head, but with a different scenario than what had played out. In my newly imagined version of events, the neighbour kept his mouth shut about the use of the property gate, and Joseph Stark was true to his offer. The End.

If I keep telling myself that this is what happened, I might start to believe it.

‘Hey beautiful lady,’ says Matt, his voice husky and rough with sleep. He slips his strong arms around me from behind and kisses my neck.

Our sex life, once Matt had healed, almost immediately picked up where we left off. It’s nice to have intimacy again, although the first few times I couldn’t help but tense up and picture what I’d done with Jace, or worse, imagine the men now able to watch the video on subscription.

One night, when I couldn’t sleep, I sat alone in the kitchen trying to find the video, googling various versions of ‘real estate agent having sex with client’ to no avail. Joseph’s porn site must be highly secure. Either that, or perhaps there’s something he does so that the videos can’t be shared or duplicated. For which I’m grateful.

I turn around and smile up at my husband. ‘Coffee?’

‘Please,’ Matt says, pecking my check then letting me go and leaning against the breakfast bench. ‘I’m going to need it for the big drive.’

For a moment I stop and think, but I can’t recall Matt mentioning anything about us going anywhere.

‘Big drive where?’

‘I’ve got a checkup appointment in the city. Remember? This is the big one. The one I get signed off on.’ He does a little celebratory wiggle and I smile, so happy that he can actually do it, that he can move his body so freely now.

‘Damn, I must have forgotten. I’m supposed to be filming and uploading my latest recipe today,’ I say, handing him a steaming mug of coffee. ‘But I can push it back until tomorrow.’

‘Oh...’ Matt grimaces at me then takes long sip of his coffee.

‘What?’

He sighs. ‘I’m actually planning on going up myself. My AA group is planning a meet up so... some of them I’ve never met face to face before... and I knew you were going to be busy with your baking stuff so I thought it was a good time to go up for the night myself and kill two birds with one stone.'

'Oh, okay. That's fine,' I say, waving his concern away, even though the idea of spending the night out here alone, so close to the forest his nan died in, sends a cold shiver running through me. 'It'll be good for you to finally put names to faces.' I force a smile. 'So it's just the one night?'

'Yeah. Are you sure that you're okay with this? Because you don't look okay.'

'It's fine, but...'

'But what?'

'I just would have thought staying away for the night would be something you'd let me know in advance about.' I rub the back of my neck. 'It's going to be the first time I'm staying out here on my own. I could have arranged for Misha to come and stay.'

I try to stifle the feeling of dread rising in my stomach. Although we've heard crickets from my stalker since we moved here, I can't help but be frightened by the idea of him suddenly showing up while Matt's away. But, of course, I can't mention this to Matt because it'll trigger his fears and overprotectiveness of me, which is the last thing I want. And I really would have liked to have caught up with my friend Misha. 'Albany is only an hour and a half away. She would have loved to come up and see me.'

Matt's cheeks tint pink and he gives me a sheepish look. 'Sorry. I may have forgotten to tell you.' He winces. 'But I'll make it up to you when I'm back, I promise. Breakfast in bed for a week.'

I grin. The last thing I want is for us to be fighting before we part. 'Now you're talking. You've got yourself a deal.'

'You want me to call Misha for you? Explain that you have a stupid husband and beg her to come stay with you?'

'Nah, I should be fine. I do have a lot to do, so I may as well make use of the husband-free time.'

'Oi.' He laughs and reaches out to tickle me, but I slip free from his grasp and rinse out my empty coffee mug. After I set it to dry on the rack, I turn around to face him.

'There was a cake recipe I was going to try, one of your nan's actually. I found it in her recipe book.' I look at Matt, hoping he doesn't think I've been purposely snooping through her personal things. But it's hard not to, when the house is still filled with her stuff. 'That is, if you don't mind me using it.'

'Of course not.' He shuffles forward and wraps his arms around me, kissing me on the forehead. 'I'm so proud of you. Your cooking thing has taken off so quickly.' He grins and waggles his eyebrows. 'I've always dreamed of being married to a hot influencer and being a kept man.'

I give him a light shove but he wraps his arms tighter around me and begins to tickle my ribs.

'Oi,' I say, between laughs. 'I'm not an influencer. I've never even showed my face in a single one of my posts and I don't intend to.'

'Are you sure about that? Next you'll be getting fillers and trout lips and taking photos in string bikinis.'

He tickles me until we both land in a twisted, laughing heap on the floor. It takes us a minute to catch our breaths and recover. This is why I did what I did in Busselton. To laugh like this with my husband again.

'Wow,' Matt says, grinning at our entwined bodies. 'Six months ago, I never would have guessed I'd be able to twist my body into a pretzel like this.'

'It's actually insane,' I say, before pressing my lips to his. 'And I'm so happy for you.'

'It's all thanks to you,' he says, looking deep into my eyes. 'You made this possible, Nadia. You.'

I wave his words away then get up and busy myself in the kitchen, lining the counter with all the ingredients I need for the cake I'll be baking today, so that I don't have to look into my husband's eyes.

Something warm brushes against my leg and I bend down and pick up Swifty, who happily purrs in my arms.

She's probably the best gift Maida Freeman left us, even better than this house. I never had a pet growing up, and the love I feel for this furry grey cat is enormous. Swifty came into Maida's life as a stray not long before she passed away. Luckily the next door neighbour kept Swifty fed and looked out for her until we took over the property. Now she's a very content cat and enjoys being spoilt by me and Matt, who loves her just as much as I do.

I bury my face in her fur, which is therapy for me, then set her down and get a bag of treats from the pantry. I give the bag a shake. 'Does Swifty want some treats?' I ask and she spins around, meowing, her fluffy tail upright as she performs her little happy dance.

I pour a few into my hand and let her eat them straight out of my palm.

'Are you alright?' Matt asks. 'Sometimes you get this look in your eyes. Like you're frightened of something.'

I force a laugh, but it comes out shaky and weak.

'Um, how about you go and pack. I need to get working on this cake so that I can put that precious husband-free time to good use and read that new romance novel I've been dying to start.'

Matt laughs and reaches over to pat Swifty's fur. Then he gets to his feet and raises his palms at me. 'Okay, okay. I promise I'll be out of your hair as soon as possible.'

I laugh too. But in truth I find it strange that Matt is spending a night in the city and leaving me out here all alone.

Matt usually doesn't let me out of his sight. Since we moved out here, he's been extra protective of me. He keeps telling me he's just worried that my stalker has followed us to Saltbush Bay, and he doesn't like that I'm so vulnerable and isolated out here in the country.

So that's why I find it odd that he's suddenly fine with leaving me alone for the night.

Which makes me wonder just who exactly he is meeting in the city.

16

Half an hour later, I'm standing on the front lawn, waving at Matt as he drives away for the night. I'm also waving away our only vehicle and thus my only way of getting into town should I decide I need something from the shops.

We haven't gotten around to getting another car and, to tell you the truth, after moving here, I didn't think we'd ever need a second car. Seeing as we usually go into town together if we need anything.

Until now, that is.

Our closest neighbour, George, is a good five-minute walk away. Not so bad on a nice sunny day like today. But I pray that I never have to run next door for help when I'm home alone at night. I'd be terrified of running into a spider web, or worse, my stalker. But I highly doubt he knows where I am. We'd stayed at several caravan parks before we moved down here. There's no way he would be able to trace me to Saltbush Bay.

A bird screeches from somewhere in the forest at the back of the house, the sound echoing across the vast land that surrounds me, reminding me that I'm truly alone right now. Goosebumps prickle my arms, but I rub them away and tilt my face towards the warm sun. It's a beautiful day and I plan to make the most of the gorgeous weather.

First, I go back inside and get to work on baking that cake. While the oven is preheating, I cream the butter and sugar, then add eggs – from our own hens – then the milk and the flour and a few drops of vanilla essence. Lastly, I grate an entire apple and crush some walnuts and add it to the batter. I pour it all into a tin and pop it in the oven, setting a timer for one hour. Which gives me enough time to pop out and collect some of those decorative flowers that carpet the forest floor.

I step out onto the back porch and pull on my boots. Although I've got my phone in my pocket, the signal is so bad out here that there are patches where we get no bars. And we still don't have our home internet set up yet – Maida didn't believe in the internet. But still, I feel safer having it with me.

The sun's warmth is comforting against my back as I exit the property gate and walk through the long grass towards the forest. I'm glad I'm wearing my long rubber boots. Although the weather is still fairly cool in the mornings, I'm still paranoid about snakes. I'm not looking forward to next month, which, according to Matt, is when baby snakes hatch from their eggs and start slithering all over the property.

When I reach the fringe of the forest, I notice that the flowers Matt and I had seen when out for our afternoon walk yesterday are all gone. Maybe our neighbour, George, picked them. Or maybe one of the other locals. I'll have to remember to tell Matt, and to ask him who else lives around here.

I glance behind me to our house in the distance and turn back to stare into the forest, where I can see plenty of purple, white and pink flowers carpeting the floor there. My heart beats wildly as I take a step forward, then another. On the third step I leave my companion, the sun, behind and shiver as I step beneath the shadowy branches of the tall old trees.

I'm not sure what exactly I'm afraid of. Maida's ghost? If ghosts were real, then I'm sure she'd have another go at me for stealing her 'Matty'.

I glance behind me once more and stare longingly at the house, the clouds of smoke puffing out of the chimney making it appear extra cosy. Matt kindly made a fire for me before he left, so that I can relax in front of it later with my romance novel. Swifty loves the fire too. I'm sure she's in there right now, curled up in front of it on the couch.

I stare at the flowers. Why do they have to be so far away?

But I tell myself that I just need to pick a few. Then I can run home and lock myself inside the house with Swifty and my book for the rest of the day.

Spurred on by that thought, I move deeper into the forest, the damp leaves a spongy carpet beneath my boots. When I reach the flowers, which are haloed by a single stream of sunlight entering through a gap in the trees, I crouch down to pluck a few of the prettier ones. I'm about to stand when something crackles up ahead.

Matt once told me that there are wild pigs out here in the bush. He said that if you didn't get in their way, you were safe.

The crackling moves closer.

The hair on my scalp prickles.

I decide I have enough flowers and go to turn and head for home when something rustles to my left.

I freeze, but when I spy a tiny blue bird dancing around on a nearby branch, I breathe a sigh of relief. It's just a bird. There are probably hundreds of little creatures living in this forest.

I smile at it. 'Hello, little friend.'

The bird fluffs up is feathers as a cool breeze snakes its way through the trees, then takes flight and disappears into the stream of sunlight.

A twig snaps somewhere in front of me, but I'm momentarily blinded from staring into the light.

Hot blood thumps through my ears.

'Hello?'

Another twig snaps, a little closer now.

I take a step back, then another, and then I turn and run.

I've almost made it to the fringe of the forest when the tip of my left boot catches on a raised, gnarled tree root and I'm sent skidding across the damp forest floor, my face smeared with sludge from the decomposing leaves

Without looking back, I scramble to my feet, losing my left boot in the process, and run all the way to the house. After I shut the gate, I finally allow myself a chance to catch my breath and check if there's anybody following me, ghost or beast or human.

But there's nothing and nobody chasing me.

I breathe a sigh of relief.

When I open my palm, I'm disappointed to find that most of the flowers I'd picked have been crushed in my rush to escape the forest. But two, one purple and one white flower have managed to remain intact, so I take them with me inside and set them on the counter for later.

I go around the entire house, making sure that all windows and doors are closed and locked, the I head into the kitchen where the delicious scent of baking fills the room.

From the very back of the pantry, behind my olive oil and vinegar bottles, I take the bottle of cooking sherry I keep hidden there from Matt, and fill a water glass with it. Now that Matt is strictly alcohol-free, we don't keep any proper drinking alcohol in the house. That's why I had to hide this bottle, which I normally only use for cooking purposes. It's too tempting for him. He's fine with me ordering a wine if we go out to the local pub for a meal, but the house needs to be booze-free, which is totally understandable.

I gulp down the sherry like it's water and sigh with satisfaction as the burn of the alcohol begins its journey through my veins, warming me from the inside out.

Feeling more relaxed now, I tidy up the kitchen and busy myself with the dishes, and before I know it, the alarm on my oven goes off and the cake is ready.

I take plenty of photos of the cake while it's still in the tin, then of it turned out on the wire rack. Later after it has cooled, I slather it with cream cheese icing and decorate it with the surviving purple and white flowers, then I present it on one of Maida's antique cake plates. It looks amazing, and I take as many snaps as I can, from different angles, the natural sunshine outside providing all the light I need.

Done. I shove my phone into my pocket. I can edit the photos later. The posts that get my best engagement are usually the ones I upload in evenings, when the rest of the world wakes up.

The sherry is doing its job. I roll my shoulders and stretch my arms and yawn. I feel completely and utterly relaxed. Now I can enjoy that husband-free time I was joking with Matt about earlier.

I heat up the leftovers from last night's dinner – roast potatoes slathered in gravy – and make myself a cup of tea to go with it. Then I go into my bedroom and fossick around for the romance novel I got at the local newsagents last week and finally plonk myself on the couch.

I turn on the telly and give Netflix at try, using my mobile phone hotspot for the internet connection. While it's attempting to load, I read a bit of my novel, then message Misha and let her know that I'm spending my first night alone. She responds, equally annoyed that Matt didn't let me know in advance so that she could have driven up to stay.

We message back and forth for a few more minutes with Misha ending the message with an offer for me to come down and spend a weekend with her in Albany for her birthday next week – which I gladly accept. It'll do me good to get out of town and away from the property for a while. Matt's getting his me-time, so I deserve some of my own.

Swifty curls up on my lap and the two of us keep each other warm as the wind picks up outside, howling through the chimney.

I must have nodded off, because the sky is darker when I wake, and Swifty is gone.

And someone is banging on my door.

17

Before I answer the door, I creep into the bedroom and carefully peel the curtains back only a few millimetres with my fingers so that I can spy on my visitor through the window – a very dusty window that I've been meaning to clean since we moved in.

Standing at the door is a woman with pale skin and shiny black hair who looks around my age, perhaps a few years older. She's wearing a flannelette shirt and is carrying a large basket filled with something that has been draped with a checkered tea towel.

I'm not usually one for chatty neighbours but I can hardly leave her standing at the door when she's gone to so much effort. A quick glance at the driveway and up and down the street confirms that she arrived on foot.

As I unlock the door, I get another look at her through the peephole and catch her smiling up at it. I duck, my heart pounding despite knowing that there is no way that she could have seen me. Forcing a smile to my face, I open the door.

'Hello,' I say, through the screen door, the fresh scent of baked goods finding its way to my nose. Whatever she's made, it smells delicious.

'Hi. I'm Annette from next door.' She raises the basket a little. 'I baked you a fresh batch of muffins.' Her nose twitches and she sniffs the air. 'But it smells like you're making something delicious yourself.'

I smile. 'Thank you. Are you... are you my–'

'Your neighbour? Yes.' She clears her throat. 'I live with George. It's only early days though,' she says, smiling shyly and shrugging her shoulders.

I unlock the screen door and step aside.

'Come in. I'm Nadia.'

'Thank you, Nadia,' she says before stepping inside.

I show her through to the kitchen.

'Wow this place looks great,' she says, her vivid green eyes popping. 'I like what you've done with the place.'

'Oh, did you know Maida? She was my husband's grandmother. And thanks,' I add, even though we've barely had the time to make any significant changes yet.

'I did,' says Annette, who sets the basket down on the kitchen counter and gazes across at the living room to where I've got a Netflix rom-com frozen on the screen. 'But Maida mainly kept to herself.'

The fire crackles cosily.

'So, what made you move all the way out here to the middle of nowhere?' she asks, smiling. 'Are you doing one of those sea-change things? I'm hearing a lot about that lately. So many people are giving up city life, or life in the suburbs, for a more peaceful and simpler way of life.'

I hesitate before answering. Annette lives out here in the middle of nowhere, so I can understand her curiosity. I'm the new shiny thing in town. But I'm hesitant to give away too much about myself. I've learned to never trust too many people with my private details. Receiving parcels in the mail from my stalker is something I never want to have to go through again. It's such a luxury to be able to go to the Saltbush Bay post office and collect my mail knowing that I'm not going to find something unwelcome waiting for me.

'Yeah. Something like that,' I say. 'My husband grew up with his grandmother, and after she passed away we decided to come out and live here, at her property. I work from home so it was an easy decision.'

'Oh, what do you do?' Annette's eyes shift to the cake set up on the kitchen bench, the empty teacups beside it for decoration. 'A food photographer?'

'Something like that.' I'm quick to change the subject. 'So what do you do?'

Nobody knows my Instagram handle, apart from Matt, and that's the way I like it. I'm not about to just hand over that kind information to anyone, even my neighbour. Matt doesn't even follow my account, just in case the stalker is checking through his follower list, searching for me.

Annette's pale cheeks tint pink. 'I'm a homemaker,' she says, almost in a whisper. 'But we ladies can't say that anymore, can we?' She shakes her head. 'What has the world come to?'

An awkward silence grows between us. Out the corner of my eye I can see the flash of the television screen as Netflix asks me if I'm still watching.

Annette looks at it too, then glances down at her watch.

'Oh, sorry,' she says. 'But I've got another batch of muffins on the go so I should probably leave you.' She touches her hips, which are in perfect shape. 'Not that I should be eating them anyway.'

I ignore her self-depreciating dig and show her out the door where I catch a glimpse of the dark clouds that seemed to have gathered out of nowhere after such a beautifully sunny day.

'I hope you get home before it rains,' I say, grimacing at the sky. 'I'd drive you home if I had a car, but my husband has taken it into the city.'

'Oh, so you're going to be all alone tonight?' she asks and shivers. 'I can come back after my muffins are done. Keep you company.'

'No need,' I say, horrified at the thought. 'I've got some work to do so I need to get stuck into that.'

'Okie doke,' she says. 'I'd better be off.'

'Be careful,' I warn, thinking about the noise I heard in the woods earlier. 'And thank you again for the muffins. It was really kind of you to bring them over.'

She snorts and steps outside.

'Trust me. It's as safe as houses out here.' She turns and grins at me. 'People are lazy these days. Even the crims have gotten slack. They aren't going to bother trekking out here in the middle of nowhere, especially when it's raining.'

'Well, that's good to know,' I say.

After we say our goodbyes, I watch her walk up the driveway and step onto the road, then I lock the screen door and close and lock the wooden door, praying that Annette dropping in unannounced doesn't become a habit. She seems nice. But I've learned to tightly guard my privacy and my free time.

Swifty appears and does figure eights between my legs.

Truth be told, I'd be happy if I never saw another soul in my life and grow old with only Matt and Swifty for company. They're all I need. If only cats could live as long as humans then I'd be all set.

'It's time for your yum-yums, isn't it?' I ask her. She's a clever cat, and understands what yum-yum means, so she happily trots toward her bowl.

After I've fed Swifty, I abandon Netflix and the novel, and decide to make a start on sorting through the junk in the spare room. Matt said that I can turn it into an office and a studio, so I'm excited to get the room cleared.

It's filled with Maida's stuff. When we first moved in, we used this room as the I-don't-know-where-this-crap-belongs-but-I'll-just-dump-it-in-here-for-now room. It has the best natural lighting in the house, so I have plans to set a dining table in the middle so that I can stage and take my photos in here.

I get started on the boxes of newspapers. Surely Matt doesn't want to keep those. I'm surprised he even took the time to shift them in here instead of tossing the lot into the recycling bin.

It takes forever to carry the boxes out to the side of the house where we keep our bins and of course the last box breaks and a pile of newspapers falls at my feet through the bottom. I groan and bend down to collect them, swearing when the wind picks up and starts blowing lose pages around the yard.

Thank God nobody is around to see me running about the property like a mad woman, making sure I've collected every single piece of newspaper. I hate the thought of littering this beautiful countryside that is home to so many wild creatures.

Once I've got it all in the bin, I notice a page from *The West Australian* that I missed, wedged beneath the box. When I bend down to pick it up, I can't help but notice the headline of an article, printed in bold letters.

WOMAN DEAD. DRIVER FIGHTING FOR LIFE.

But it's not the headline that quickens my pulse, it's the picture below it.

Of a car.

Not just any car.

Jace's shiny black sports car.

Although the license plate has been blurred, the car is unmistakable. The customised spoiler on the back, and the special LED lights that he told me he'd had installed right after he bought it.

I check the date and my blood runs cold.

April.

A month after I'd slept with him.

I read the article. According to the police, the car hit a bridge pillar at over one hundred and twenty kilometres per hour. It says that his female passenger, who I presume to be his wife, died on impact. Did Jace survive the accident?

I dig back through the other newspapers, specifically the ones dated after the accident, but find no other mention of it.

So I head back inside and lock the door behind me.

It's time to start googling.

18

Of course my phone has decided to go flat. So I plug it in and while I wait for it to charge, I put the kettle on and make myself a cup of tea.

While I sit at the kitchen bench at sip my tea, I keep staring at the grainy photograph in the article that I brought inside with me. No matter how many times I study it, I come to the same terrible conclusion. It's definitely Jace's car. He has one hundred percent been involved in a fatal accident.

I put a hand to my mouth at the horror of it all. Had what we'd done in Busselton finally gotten to him? Had he driven into the bridge pillar because he couldn't stand to live with the guilt anymore?

No. He loved his wife. I remember how tortured he was that night, at the idea of hurting her. There's no way he'd do that to her. Himself, maybe. But not his beautiful wife.

Once the phone is sufficiently charged, I unplug it and take it with me to the couch and begin scouring the net for articles. Swifty hops up onto my lap and curls up into a contented, purring ball, and I stroke her grey, striped fur as I click on each of the three articles I've found. But I'm disappointed when I discover that they are all nearly identical to the newspaper article. Next, I google Jace's real estate agency and I bring a hand to my mouth when I see that it is listed as *Permanently Closed.*

Swifty glances up at me, as though sensing that something is wrong. I stroke her fur and she settles again.

I log onto Instagram and search Jace's name and my stomach flutters when I find his user tag @TheRealEstateJace100. I've been working so hard at forcing Jace out of my mind for the past six months, that seeing his smiling face in his profile pic stops my heart. I blink, feeling a wave of sadness, then exhale and click on his most recent post.

His last uploaded photo is a scenic mountain and lake view along with a motivational quote, the kind that rich people and successful corporate types typically post.

I check the date.

April 13th.

Nothing has been posted since then.

I click on the comments and find an endless stream of crying emojis and broken hearts, and my head feels light. Along with the business no longer operating, I can only conclude that he died from his injuries.

I scroll down to a photo of him and his wife at a gala event. She's so beautiful with her long blonde hair and sparkling blue eyes.

I click on the tagged username and start scrolling through her page. The last photo she posted is a #flashbackfriday of a holiday in Broome she and Jace took the year before. It's of the Staircase to the Moon phenomenon. The tag at the bottom of the photo says #takemeback and it brings a tear to my eyes. Like Jace's last photo, there is an endless stream of crying emojis and broken hearts.

My blood runs cold when I check the date. April the thirteenth. I scroll back and see that she'd posted daily up until this date. An endless stream of bright and colourful photos of a beautiful woman who seemingly lived her life to the full and enjoyed the luxuries that her husband's income had to offer.

Which can only mean one thing. That she's dead.

That poor woman. And poor Jace. Two lives destroyed just like that in an instant. Maybe it was a death wish, or maybe it was purely accidental. Jace loved to speed. He was likely going too fast and lost control. What a tragedy.

I close the app and toss my phone onto the couch, tears stinging my eyes.

The only good thing to have come from this – and I feel terribly guilty for even thinking it – is that my secret has died with Jace.

19

Sleep doesn't come easily. But that's what I get for camping out on the couch for the night and having Swifty use me as a human pillow. Not that the lack of comfort is responsible for my insomnia. It's pure fear.

I keep hearing footsteps outside, leaves crunching beneath boot heels, and I can't help imagining that somebody – my stalker, Maida's ghost, or some stranger – is creeping around the house trying to find their way inside.

Every gust of wind, every branch scraping against the roof, the rattle of the back gate, all serve to confirm to me that a psychotic murderer is outside, just waiting for their moment to pounce.

When I finally manage to fall asleep, Jace and his wife haunt my dreams. Lying broken in the mangled wreck of the shiny black sports car, they both reach for me with bruised and bloody arms. And when Jace finally catches hold of me, his fingers digging into my skin, he looks into my eyes and says, in a raspy demonic growl, *we made a big mistake, Nadia, and we're going to hell for it.*

That's when I wake up, my heart pounding loud enough to stir Swifty, who is curled up on my chest. She gets up and stretches across my torso before hopping onto the floor and padding across the polished wooden boards to stick her fluffy head around the thick curtains. I follow suit and take a peek.

The sky is a silvery purple, and although the sun is not yet up, the birds have begun their morning song. It's comforting. One of my favourite things about living in the country is the abundant birdlife we have here. I've ordered an Australian bird book online so that I can begin documenting which species visit the property.

I turn the coffee machine on and while it's brewing, I take a shower. As I lather up the shampoo in my hair, I feel as though I'm washing away all the uneasiness that I've felt for the past twenty-four hours.

Twenty minutes later, I'm wearing a comfy bamboo pant and long sleeve top set and sitting on the couch watching the sunrise through the open curtains.

Swifty sits beside me, *eekeekeeking* at the birds she can see dancing atop the banksia shrubs outside the window. I roll my shoulders and stroke Swifty's soft grey fur, and with each sip of coffee, I feel the tension from last night melting away.

Everything looks better in the morning. Maybe the noise I'd heard out in the forest yesterday was a local out for a walk, searching for flowers like me. And as for Jace and his wife... It's unfortunate what happened. But it wasn't a guilty conscience or karma that ended their lives. Judging by how fast Jace drove his car, it was likely speed that killed them.

I need to do my best to forget all about them and what happened that night six months ago. I've already screwed up the newspaper article and stuffed it under the pre-stacked kindling in the fireplace, ready for today's fire. Hopefully the ceremony of burning the article might help me to put it all behind me.

By the time Matthew arrives home, late in the afternoon, I've baked four trays of biscuits – one each of Anzacs, pecan dainties, macadamia and white chocolate chip, and my famous cornflake cookies as well as an almond orange cake.

'Something smells amazing,' Matt calls as he enters through the back door. *Nobody uses the front door out here in the country*, he told me when we first moved in.

I set my oven mitts aside and meet him in the laundry for a big hug. He squeezes me tight and pecks my forehead. 'You're a sight for sore eyes.'

'I missed you too,' I say, unsure if I want to mention the noise in the forest and the fact that I've left a boot out there. He'll probably worry that my stalker has found me and glue himself to my side. And anyway, I'm looking forward to spending some girlie time with Misha.

I bury my face into his neck and freeze when I notice a new scent. Something sweet and floral, completely unlike the aftershave he wears.

'Is that perfume?' I ask, pulling away.

He looks at me and laughs. 'Perfume?' He frowns and thinks for a moment, then his brows shoot up beneath his dark fringe. 'Oh, it must be the hotel body wash. Manuka honey and raspberry seed or something like that.' He makes a face.

I smile and pretend to laugh it off, but deep inside my heart is fluttering with worry. Matt's online AA chat group has been good for him, and likely saved him during his darkest days, but sometimes I wonder about how much time he spends on there, and just who he's chatting with. Of course, I can't blame him for growing close to the members of his chat group – sharing private details of your struggles with addiction must create a sense of intimacy between them that can't be matched in the outside world. Even I can't fully understand and appreciate what Matt went through while he was stuck at home in the apartment unable to work or even perform simple household tasks. He'd once cried out in pain and collapsed to the floor when he'd attempted to fold a basket of washing.

But the scent of that perfume bothers me and makes me wonder if he did in fact meet with his AA group last night.

'I'm going to unpack and take a shower.'

'Okay,' I say, hiding my suspicions with a smile.

A little while later, Matt dressed in a fresh pair of dark jeans and a corduroy shirt, enters the kitchen and watches me pack the biscuits away in his grandmother's old Tupperware containers.

'Gosh I remember the rock cakes my nan used to make. She always put them in that orange container.'

I smile at my husband. His hair is damp and has curled, as it always does when wet. 'I love these containers too. They remind me of my mum.' I don't have many memories of my mum, but I'll never forget her Tupperware collection. 'When she cooked, she used to open up the bottom cupboard and let me take out the containers and lids and make a mess,' I say, my heart warming at the memory, even though it's gauzy at best. I was only four when my mother passed away from an aneurysm.

Matt knows I don't have many memories of my mum, and comes around the counter to give me hug.

'How about you go and get yourself ready for dinner at the pub,' he says, pressing his lips to my cheek. 'Tonight's the garlic prawn special.'

My stomach growls in response and I tear myself out of his grasp, the perfume forgotten.

'Yay. I'll be quick.' I race into the bedroom to strip out of my bamboo lounge set and slip on a white maxi dress, a coral cardi on top, and a pair of white sneakers.

'You look cute,' says Matt when I return to the kitchen, his eyes all starry.

'So do you,' I say, coming to straighten his collar. 'Is that a new shirt?'

His cheeks blush lightly. 'Yeah. I got it in Freo.'

'Nice,' I say, not liking the way that his cheeks tinted pink. Matt is definitely keeping something from me. But tonight is not the night to ask questions. I'll save my investigations for tomorrow.

For now, however. I just want a nice night out with my husband, to drown myself in creamy garlic sauce and block out what I've learned in the past twenty-four hours.

'Let's go,' he says, grinning.

20

We're early, but already the pub is busy. The garlic prawn special is legendary in these parts and we've met people who have travelled down from the city just to try them.

I manage to nab our favourite booth while Matt goes to get our drinks. They have a decent selection of non-alcoholic beers, which is great for him. While I'm waiting, I don't bother with the menu because we know what we're having, so instead I partake in a little bit of people-watching. It's one of my favourite pastimes.

I spy a couple with two small children and smile as I watch the dad who is helping his daughter to tie her hair back so that she can eat her nuggets and chips without dipping her hair into the tomato sauce. Meanwhile the mum is carefully positioning the son's soft toy so that the toddler can see it at all times whilst he's eating his spaghetti. It warms my heart and makes me wonder what Matt and I would be like as parents.

Matt's not back yet and when I crane my neck over the top of the booth I can see that he's speaking to an older man at the bar who is wearing an Akubra hat so worn that the crown has frayed away to reveal a head of thick grey hair.

'Who was that?' I ask, when Matt returns with his alcohol-free beer and my large glass of white wine.

'Oh, I should have introduced you. That's our neighbour, George. He's been over east for his daughter's wedding and got back yesterday. It was his first holiday since his wife died.'

'Aww. That's sweet and so sad too.'

'Well, he's happy that we've moved into my nan's place. He said it gets pretty lonely out there all by himself.'

'You mean the next-door neighbour that you said is a five minute walk away?'

'Yep,' says Matt smiling and frowning at the same time. 'What's that weird look on your face for?'

I take a sip of my wine and set the glass down on the coaster.

'How old is he roughly?'

Matt shrugs. 'I don't know, seventy maybe?'

I put a hand to my mouth. 'Well, I just happened to meet his girlfriend yesterday while you were away.'

'Girlfriend?' Matt frowns. 'No way. George is still grieving his wife. He isn't the type to move on like that.'

'But she knocked on our door and gave me a basket of muffins.'

Matt draws his head back and throws me a look of disbelief. 'Really?' He frowns before he takes a sip of his beer and shakes his head. 'I can't believe that he's moved on so quickly. They were a proper golden couple. All loved up even in their later years.'

'Maybe it's out of pure loneliness,' I say.

'What's she look like?'

I shrug. 'Dark hair and vivid green eyes. She's significantly younger,' I add, my eyebrows dancing.

Matt laughs and reaches across the table for my hand, and I can't help but wonder if I'm letting my imagination get the better of me with the perfume and the new shirt. If he was truly seeing another woman, then surely he wouldn't be so affectionate with me.

'So why didn't you tell me about the visit?' Matt asks, his smile slowly disappearing.

I shrug. 'I don't know. I saw you for all of five minutes before you told me to go get ready for dinner so I've hardly had the time.'

He looks at me, his hazel eyes dark with seriousness. 'You need to tell me if someone visits. Especially after what happened back home.'

'I know, but when you convinced me to move out here, you said it was a safer place to live than the city or the suburbs.'

'Yes, and I stand by what I said. I meant for normal everyday people, Saltbush Bay and the surrounding areas is a safe place to live. But you have a stalker, so your situation is anything but normal.'

I take a sip of wine and maybe it's the alcohol, but I decide to tell him about the forest and the noises I heard in there.

'You left the house while I wasn't home?' Matt asks, his eyes nearly popping out of his head. 'Are you insane? If your stalker had shown up, I wouldn't have been there to protect you. And my grandmother died in those woods.'

An elderly couple at a nearby table glance at us.

'Stop raising your voice,' I hiss at him. 'People are staring.'

'So let them,' he says, glaring at the nearby tables.

The elderly couple begin talking to each other, actively avoiding eye contact with Matt. I want to sink beneath the booth table.

'It was probably just an animal,' I say, keeping my voice calm and wishing now that I'd never mentioned it. 'You told me that there are wild pigs out there.'

'Trust me, you'd know if it was a wild pig.' He shakes his head. 'Jesus, Nadia. I thought I could trust you to be sensible when you're on your own, but I can see now that I can't.'

I raise my brows. 'Well actually, Misha invited me down to Albany next weekend. It's her birthday so we're going to have a nice girlie weekend together. I'll need to borrow the car though.'

Matt's face turns to stone. 'Absolutely not. It's not safe for you to travel to Albany alone. I've only been gone for one night and already you've answered the door to a stranger and gone out wandering in the middle of nowhere.'

'You make it sound like I'm going off to war. She's my best friend and I want to see her. I may be your wife, but you don't own me, Matt. You don't get to tell me what to do.'

'I'm only looking out for you, Nadia. And anyway, you can't take the car next weekend.'

'Why?'

'It's booked in to get the brakes done. I noticed they were making a grinding noise while I was away, so I booked it in online. Sorry.' He takes a glug of his alcohol-free beer and starts reading the menu even though we both know we want the special.

'I'm going to the bathroom,' I announce, before I say something that I regret.

In the ladies room I stare at myself in the mirror and press some cold water to my flushed cheeks.

I get that Matt is only being protective of me, but it's frustrating that he gets to spend the night away and bath in manuka honey and raspberry seed body wash, and buy himself a new shirt, when I have to stay home because 'it's not safe'.

After five minutes tick by, I'm about to leave when a black-haired woman enters the bathroom.

'Annette?' I say, looking at her pale reflection in the mirror. I turn around and she jolts slightly, as though I've scared her.

'Oh sorry. You're the new neighbour...' She frowns at me. 'What was your name again?' She looks into the mirror and runs a hand through her dark, wavy hair, fluffing it up. 'I've got the worst memory I'm afraid.'

'Nadia,' I say, thinking how weird this is. She's a completely different person to the overly friendly woman who visited me yesterday with the basket of muffins. 'I just saw your partner, George. He was chatting to my husband. Are you two here for the garlic prawn special?'

Annette blinks rapidly and then smiles. 'Yes. The prawns are amazing, aren't they?'

I nod and then we stare at each other awkwardly until Annette puts a hand to her head. 'Actually. If you'll excuse me, I'm feeling a bit off. I think I'm coming down with something.'

'Of course. I'll leave you to it.' I smile at her over my shoulder as I leave. 'See you around.'

Annette nods. Her face pale. She doesn't look good at all.

'You won't believe who I just saw in the loos,' I say when I sit back down opposite Matt at the booth. 'George's girlfriend. But she said she's not feeling well.'

'Really? You need to point her out to me when she comes out.' The shift of focus onto George's girlfriend seems to have brightened Matt's mood and dissolved any lingering tension between us.

'I'll go order the prawns,' I say, and head to the bar.

While I'm ordering, I notice George sitting over at a corner table, his back to me and I contemplate heading over to introduce myself, but then Annette exits the ladies room and I watch her go to his table and bend down to speak into his ear. Then she grabs her handbag and rushes out of the pub with a hand over her mouth.

I pay for the two servings of prawns and rush back to Matt.

'I just saw her. Annette, George's girlfriend. But she left.'

'She's done a runner, hey?' Matt shakes his head. 'Poor old George. How old do you think this woman is?'

I shrug. 'A couple of years older than us maybe? Mid-thirties?'

A waitress delivers our steaming plates of rice smothered in creamy garlic prawns and we thank her.

'Yum,' I say, picking up my fork.

'Wow. George is in his seventies. That's around a forty-year age gap. I hope she's not taking advantage of him. He's a real soft touch and is the kind of bloke that would give a person the last shirt off his back.' Matt frowns. He looks genuinely troubled. 'I'll have to keep a close eye on him.'

Just like you do me, I want to say.

But instead, I shove a delicious prawn into my mouth.

21

Today Matt is working on the firebreaks, so I use the opportunity to call Misha about her birthday weekend. I take my phone into the study which has the best phone reception in the house.

'Hey, how are you?' she says as soon as she answers.

'I'm good, thanks, and you?'

'I'm great. I hope you're calling to confirm that you're coming down for my birthday.'

'Well... I'm not, *not* coming, if that makes sense. I just need more time to convince Matt that I'm not in any mortal danger by travelling alone to Albany to see you.'

'Since when do you need permission from your husband, Nadia? I can forgive him his clinginess while he was sick, but now that he's well again it's plain weird. And you're literally only an hour and a half away.'

I try my best to distract Misha by telling her all about Annette and her basket of muffins, and the offer to keep me company while Matt was away. But she doesn't take the bait.

'Let me talk to Matt,' she says.

'No. He's out doing the firebreaks anyway.'

She laughs. 'I swear to God that guy hates me.'

I clear my throat. 'To be fair, you've never actually warmed to him yourself.'

She sighs. 'True. But that's because I've always found him a bit... controlling. Maybe not so much in the beginning. But since he did his back in, it's as though he completely changed.'

'Yeah, but if you or I were in the same position he was in, maybe we wouldn't be ourselves either.'

'Fair point. But remember all those times he forgot to tell you that I called?'

'A lot of people do that. I'm always forgetting stuff. And we were in the middle of moving house so it's completely understandable.'

'But this was different. He actually went onto your phone and deleted my call notifications. That's abnormal behaviour and you know it.'

I'm silent for a few seconds. She's right. And it disturbs me that I was able to forget that major detail and pretend as though it hadn't happened.

'Okay. I'm coming.'

'What?'

'I'm coming for your birthday. I don't care what Matt says or thinks. He can't stop me,' I declare. Then I remember that the car is getting it's brakes done. 'Shit,' I mutter.

'What is it?'

'Nothing. Don't worry. I'll be there.'

Misha squeals down the other end of the line. 'I cannot wait to see you.'

'Same.' I walk over to the window and see that Matt is driving the tractor back to the shed. He must have finished already. 'Okay, I've got to go. Chat soon.'

'Bye.'

I leave the study and toss my phone onto the couch on my way to the kitchen to check on the banana bread baking in the oven. It still has at least twenty minutes to go, but it's coming along nicely. While I'm waiting for it to finish, I set up the dining table for a photo shoot, this time sprinkling some flour across the wooden surface for a rustic effect.

'Hey,' says Matt, coming up behind me.

I'd gotten so involved with the table setting that I didn't even hear him come in.

'Um, wow,' I say when I turn and get a good look at him. He's covered head to toe in thick brown dust, with only his eyes and the space where his sunglasses sat, untouched. 'Someone needs a good shower.'

'Actually I'm going to the beach for a swim. You wanna come?'

I glance at my oven and groan. Going to the beach is one of my favourite outings since we moved here. I love strolling along the shore looking for shells and other treasures while Matt takes a dip in the sea.

'Damn. The cake's not ready. Can you wait?'

He gestures to his dirt-covered body. 'Not really.'

'Well if we had another car, then I'd be able to catch up with you once the cake is done,' I say.

'By the way, I spoke with Misha.'

'Oh, okay. Did you tell her you couldn't come? That the car's going to be in the garage?'

'Actually, I told her that I'd find a way to make if down if we get another car.'

'Why would you say that? We've no need for a second car.'

I gesture towards the oven, as though waiting for the cake to bake is the most logical of reasons behind getting another car.

'Clearly we do. If we had another car, I'd be meeting you at the beach in half an hour.'

Matt frowns and shakes his head, then disappears into the laundry, slamming the back door shut behind him.

I watch him through the living room window as he takes off his boots then strips off his filthy shirt and long pants, leaving him bare-chested and dressed in a pair of blue and black board shorts.

He gets into the car and drives away.

I'm not sure that exhaling with relief after your husband leaves the house is a sign of a good marriage. But I'm not sure what to think anymore. Maybe Misha's words have gotten to me, and I'm starting to see signs of controlling behaviour where there aren't any or maybe I've been delusional all along, making excuses for Matt's behaviour because it's easier to blame it on his back injury than to admit that I might have a controlling husband.

The oven alarm bell rings and I take the banana bread out. It's perfect, and I turn it out on the wire rack to cool. Once it's cool enough, I set it up on a wooden chopping block, with a square of creamy butter on a small white dish beside it along with an antique butter knife. I'm sure my followers are going to love this one.

I take over a hundred snaps, so that I've got plenty to choose from. I like to pick the best photo possible. The realest photo. So that when my followers view it, they'll want to step inside the picture, cut themselves a slice of cake and spread the fresh butter all over it.

I start clearing the table when there's a knock at the front door. I wonder who it could be? Maybe it's Annette. I feel awful for not having done the neighbourly thing and gone over to check on her at George's place after seeing her dash off last night. I'll make it up to her by inviting her in for a cup of tea.

I take a look through the peephole in the door and freeze.

It's not Annette at all. But instead a man with a shaved head wearing dark sunglasses and a medical face mask. My pulse immediately rises.

When I don't answer, he bangs on the door again, this time with a little more force.

I make sure that the door is locked and creep away from it, before tiptoeing to the living room for my phone. Once I have it in my hands, I take it, along with Swifty who is hiding behind the couch, and lock myself in the study.

After setting Swifty down on top of the still-unpacked boxes from the move, I dial up Matthew.

He doesn't answer. Must be swimming. I swear with frustration and end the call then text him, telling him to come home immediately. That someone is at the door and that I'm frightened.

I peel the curtain aside to check if the man has entered our yard, but thankfully he hasn't, or at least, not as far as I can see.

After five agonisingly long minutes pass by with no more knocks, I'm certain that the stranger is gone. So I creep out of the room and slowly make my way through the house and down the hallway to the front door.

When I put my eye to the peephole, I gasp. Now the man is shoving a scrap of paper in our mailbox. Then I watch, my heart racing, as he gets back into his car, which is parked parallel to the side of the road. Unfortunately the angle makes me unable to get his number plate, but I take note of the kind of vehicle he's driving. It's white. A very modern-looking car. Definitely an electric one, or at least a hybrid. Not something that I'd imagine my stalker driving, but I'm not about to stereotype a stalker.

Finally, he drives away.

I want to check the mailbox but I'm also worried that it's some kind of bait to lure me out with. That he's only taken his car a little way down the road, and he's waiting to attack me once I go outside.

Where on earth is Matt? I head into the living room and open our message feed on my phone and see that he's read the message but hasn't replied.

Swifty comes to me and rubs against my leg and I bend down to scoop her up and cradle her to my chest. She purrs instantly and offers me some comfort.

A car pulls up. Matt's by the sound of it and I sigh with relief when I see him walk past the living room window to the back door.

'Are you okay?' he asks, breathlessly, his hair and shorts damp and smelling of the salty sea. 'Sorry I didn't write back. As soon as I saw your message I ran to the car and floored it all the way here.'

'I'm fine now,' I say, wrapping my arms around his waist. He hugs me tightly.

'Did you get a good look at him?'

'He had a shaved head. But he was wearing sunglasses and a face mask which covered his nose and mouth so...' I shrug. 'So I can't really say what he looks like exactly.'

Matt swears. 'I bet it's him. That bastard.'

'He left something in the mailbox,' I say. 'Let's go see what it says.'

Matt pulls away from me and grips my shoulders. '*I* will go see what it says. It's not safe for you to go outside right now.'

'Did you see any cars when you drove home? He's got an electric or hybrid white car. Something brand new.'

'No. Now stay here,' he says, and heads back outside.

I run to the bedroom where I have a good view of the front yard and watch as Matt reaches into the mailbox and pulls out the scrap of paper that the man left. My heart pounds as I watch Matt's face turn to stone when he reads it.

Then he looks up and glances around him, not noticing me at the window, and proceeds to tear the piece of paper to shreds before dropping it into the recycling bin.

'What did it say?' I ask, when he comes back in.

Matt's face is completely blank. Even his eyes look eerily emotionless.

'Nothing.'

'What do you mean?'

'I mean, it wasn't important. The guy is obviously sick in the head and very delusional.'

Matt's voice has risen so I don't push it for now. I'll prod him a little more after dinner tonight, when he's more relaxed and maybe when we're watching something on the telly.

'I was going to make pasta for dinner,' I say, hoping to defuse some of the tension in the room.

Matt nods. 'I'm taking a shower,' he says before he disappears down the hall and into the bathroom, locking the door behind him.

He usually has pretty quick showers, unlike me. But it's more than enough time for me to dash outside and try to read what's left of the note.

I wait for the old pipes to rattle through the walls, until I know for sure that he's under the shower, then head out the back door and quietly make my way to the side of the driveway where we keep the wheelie bins.

Luckily for me, the recycling bin is almost full to the top with those old newspapers I threw out yesterday, so the shredded paper is sitting in a neat pile on top. I gather the little pieces in my hand and do my best to put the note together, my pulse whooshing loudly in my ears the entire time.

Nadia is the first word I put together, then a phone number, which seems harmless enough.

But then I put the rest of the message together and my blood runs cold.

> *Nadia, please call me. It's urgent. Someone is trying to hurt you.*

22

There is no name written on the note. Just the phone number.

I take my phone out of my pocket and photograph the note for later. I'm sure there's a way to call someone with your own number hidden so I'll try that if it's possible because if that man is, in fact, my stalker, then the note could very well be a tactic that he's using to get hold of my private number.

What baffles me is the fact that Matt tore the note up instead of showing it to me and suggesting we go to the police with it. Isn't he concerned that this man could hurt us now that he knows where we live? A phone number is likely the only breakthrough that we'll ever get in finding out who this man is. Surely the police could trace it back to the owner.

We spend the rest of the day mostly outside, gardening in the glorious spring sunshine. The weather reports keep predicting rain, and although we've had some clouds gather, like that afternoon Annette came round to see me, the rain has yet to come.

Swifty has been enjoying herself outside too, chasing the field mice and trying, and failing, to catch the grasshoppers leaping around in the grass.

Matt swears suddenly and rips his glove off and inspects his finger. 'Bloody hell. I cut myself.'

'On what?'

'A bit of glass.'

'Do you want me to get a Band-Aid?'

'Nah, I'll go clean it up myself.'

I watch him leave and after he disappears inside the house, I take off my gloves and pluck my phone out of my pocket. It's full signal out here, so I'm going to take advantage. Matt has been glued to my side all day, almost as though he knows that I have the photo of the note in my phone.

But just as I'm about to dial the mystery number, I hear someone calling out.

I look up to see George waving at me. He's leaning against the fence that borders our property and is smiling, probably wanting to introduce himself. Maybe he has an update on how Annette is doing.

'Hi,' I say, when I get closer.

George takes his crownless hat off and dips his head. 'I'm George.' He says, smiling. 'And you must be the lovely Nadia that Matthew has been telling me about.'

I smile and shake his outstretched hand. 'I'm not lovely all the time, trust me.'

He laughs. 'Maida's cat's been around my yard a bit.'

'Oh, I'm sorry. I do try to keep an eye on her when she's out.'

'No, no, don't worry. It's a good thing. She's been catching the mice in my garden. She can come anytime she likes.' As if on cue, Swifty leaps up onto the fence and gives George's arm a friendly nudge with her furry little head.

'How is Annette doing?' I ask. 'I saw her at the pub the other night and she didn't look too good.'

'She's right as rain. Must have been one of those twenty-four-hour things. She's gone up to the city for a couple of nights.' George shrugs. 'Family stuff I think.'

'Oh.' An awkward silence descends between us as I think about their age difference and I feel terrible about my inner judgement because George really does seem like a lovely man. 'So how long have the two of you been together?'

'Together?' George throws his head back and laughs. 'You didn't think that Annette and I...' He shakes his head vigorously. 'Oh God no. She's just my housekeeper. House-sitter actually. She moved in to look after my place when I went over east for my kid's wedding. She's young enough to be my daughter. No. No.' He smiles at me and his lined face softens. 'I'm a faithful man to my dear late wife and I intend to be until I see her again.'

George's eyes are shining with unshed tears and I'm moved by his love for his wife. There's not much of that around these days. Not with dating apps and direct messages making it all too easy for those inclined to cheat. I hope that Matt and I have a long and loving relationship like what George seems to have had with his wife.

'My mistake,' I say. 'I just assumed when she came around that she was your partner.'

'Oh don't worry about it,' he says, grinning. 'At least you gave this old man a good laugh today.'

I smile and then I notice a car sitting in his shed with a cover draped over it.

'That car is not for sale by any chance, is it?' I ask.

He looks at it for a long time.

'It's my Amy's car,' he says, his voice distant sounding. 'It's not for sale.' He swallows and looks back at me. 'But I tell you what. You can use it any time you like. I know you've only got the one car and I have three. I think Amy would like her car to be driven once in a while.'

I tell George about my planned trip to Albany to visit Misha, and how our car is getting its brakes done that weekend.

He claps his hands together. 'You must borrow Amy's car. I insist. And I know that Amy'd want you to get to Albany for your friend's birthday. My wife loved catching up with her friends. It was important to her and she always returned happy and glowing from spending time with them, which was a bonus for me.' He chuckles. 'I myself visit the Men's Shed just out of town. Once a week me and the local blokes meet up and have a good yarn and more than a few laughs. It's good for the soul.'

'Nadia!'

George and I turn to see Matt waving his arms frantically at me from the house.

'Oh no, he sounds grumpy,' George says, chuckling.

'I'd better go,' I say, rolling my eyes. 'And thanks for the offer to borrow the car. I promise you I'll look after it and wash it before I give it back to you. And I'll fill up the tank too.'

George waves his hat at me. 'If you do all of that then I'll have nothing left to do. Us oldies need jobs to keep us busy.'

I smile. He really is a lovely man. Hearing about how much he respected his wife's need for space only serves to emphasis just how unnatural it is for Matt to be so opposed to me visiting Misha.

'Thanks, George. I'll come to see you during the week.'

'No worries. I'll have it ready for the weekend. And anyway. I'll probably see you at the fair so we can chat about it then.'

'Okay,' I say, although I have no idea what fair he's talking about.

I leave him staring in the direction of the car, probably lost in a memory of his dear Amy.

Matt hollers at me again, but I'm too happy to feel irritated because next weekend I'll be driving down to Albany in Amy's car to visit Misha.

And nothing and no one is going to stop me.

23

In the evening, Matt tries to smooth things over by cooking me dinner.

'That looks good,' I say, coming into the kitchen to watch him plate up the steak, potato gratin and green beans, all of which are my absolute favourites.

'Sorry,' he says, smiling at me sheepishly over the steam coming off the green beans.

'For hollering at me like a neanderthal in front of George?'

Matt grimaces. 'Was it that bad?'

'Of course it was bad. What on earth possessed you to think that it's okay to shout at me like that?'

'I don't know. It's the note, and the fact that your stalker knows where we live. It's stressing me out.'

I shake my head. 'You don't get to blame your appalling behaviour on that note, which by the way, you didn't even let me read.'

'You're right,' he says, hanging his head and setting the dirty fry pan in the sink. 'It's inexcusable and I'm very sorry. Can you find it in your gloriously compassionate heart to forgive me?' He slides the plate towards me and my traitorous stomach groans.

It's no use staying mad at Matt, so I nod my head and take my plate and together we get comfy on the couch.

The food is as delicious as it looks. And after we demolish the lot, our stomachs achingly full, Matt turns the television. It's the AFL semi-finals and even though our football team hasn't made it, we settle on the couch underneath a blanket together to watch it.

We choose a team to barrack for and have fun cheering as our chosen team begins to lead in the first quarter. Matt is so relaxed right now, so different to the moody husband he was all afternoon. I'm not sure if it's because he genuinely feels bad for yelling at me in front of George, and for being so overbearing about my safety, or if it's because of the call he took on his phone just before we started to discuss what we were going to have for dinner. The more I think about it, the more I'm convinced it was the call.

He'd disappeared into the study for a good ten minutes and when he came back out, he told me he'd been speaking to one of the boys from the chat group. It was strange, though. The way he'd gone into the study fuming and glaring at me, and then had come back out whistling and announcing that he didn't need any help with dinner. That he had it covered and that I deserved to relax and chill on the couch while he cooked for me.

'Hey, can I borrow your phone?' Matt asks. 'Mine's charging in the study.'

'Oh,' I say. 'I can get yours if you like.'

'Nah,' he says, reaching across me for mine, which I left resting on the couch arm. 'I just want to quickly search up something.'

'What are you looking up?' I ask, my stomach churning with anxiety, and all that rich food I ate. I have a bad feeling he's checking my messages to Misha.

Although I planned on telling Matt over dinner about George loaning me his wife's car, I haven't gotten around to it yet. But I did get a chance to message Misha this afternoon about it, which, if Matt's snooping through my messages, he's going to find out pretty soon.

I try to focus on the television, but although my eyes are following the football players, all I can think about is Matt finding out about me going away without me having told him first. Of course, it's not a huge thing, but I can imagine that he's not going to like that I made arrangements behind his back. Even though I have every right to go. No matter how protective he is of me.

Around two minutes later, Matt hands me my phone back. I'm dying to see if he's been lazy and left an app open. But that will have to wait. I can't tell if he's seen anything he doesn't like because his face is unreadable and his eyes are glued to the television screen.

He puts an arm around me and draws me in for a cuddle. When I curl up in his arms and rest my head against his chest, he exhales, his body relaxing and his racing heart slowing to a regular beat. Hopefully he'll get tired quickly. He usually doesn't last long with a full belly and was up early this morning to do the firebreaks, so there's a good chance he'll nod off soon.

Thankfully, during the last quarter of the football game, he tips his head back against the couch and begins to snore softly. Once Matt's fallen asleep, it's usually quite difficult to wake him. Even if I take him to bed, he usually doesn't put up a fight and allows me to lead him to the bedroom where he usually flops straight onto the mattress and continues snoring. But tonight I decide to leave him snoring on the couch.

I carefully ease myself out of his arms and place a cushion there instead. He smacks his lips and snorts a little, but then settles back into a rhythmic snore.

Taking my phone with me, I head into the study and close the door behind me. The first thing I do is check my phone. He's left the search engine open but that's about it. I check the history and see that he's been looking at new tractors, something he did mention over dinner. Okay, so maybe there was nothing sinister in him borrowing my phone. But then I remember the photo of the note I'd pieced back together like a jigsaw puzzle and open my camera roll.

I swear beneath my breath.

The photo is gone.

I check the deleted folder, but it's been deleted from there too.

My pulse thunders in my ears.

Why would he delete the photo? Why would he not want to know what kind of danger I was in? If he's as protective of me as he claims, then why isn't he doing anything about it?

The hairs on the back of my neck stand on end.

My gaze is drawn to Matt's phone, charging on the study desk.

If he can snoop through my phone, then surely it's fair for me to do the same.

I enter his passcode, which is his birth year, then scroll through his messages.

There's nothing special so far. A conversation with his brother, who lives in Malaysia, is the most recent message, apart from his messages with me. Nothing suspect at all.

Then I search through his photos, but find nothing of interest there. Photos of the firebreaks are the most recent pics, and as I scroll back, I find some old selfies from when he was in hospital, the ones he'd sent to me. So nothing suspicious there either.

I'm about to put his phone back on the desk when I remember the AA forum and search his phone for the app. When I find it, I click on it and try my best to navigate the pages. Most are posts by members detailing their successes, or their failings. Matt doesn't seem to have been active on any of the message boards so I click on the little envelope icon and find myself scrolling through his direct messages.

Most seem to come from a user called MorningBird83, which I imagine is a woman, one who is a few years older than Matt if the '83 is anything to go by.

Most of their message threads seem fairly innocent. Mostly about their struggles with alcohol. They seemed to have done most of their talking during the time Matt was home with his injured back.

There are so many messages it takes a while to get through them all from the start, and although there doesn't seem to be anything sexual or romantic going on between the two, at least not on this app, I get a sense that they have developed a close relationship over the past year. The fact that there are so many messages between them, hundreds, if not thousands, leaves me feeling a little cold.

I continue to scroll, in search of what, I don't know.

Eventually my lids grow heavy and my neck becomes stiff, and I'm about to call it a night when I spy the name Jace in one of the messages.

Suddenly I'm wide awake.

I quickly scroll back to the thread where I'd spotted it and am about to read what it says when Matt bursts through the door.

'What are you doing with my phone?' he asks. His hair is messed up and his eyes are wild, making him appear unhinged.

'Oh, I just came in to see if it was charged and was going to leave it on your bedside table for the morning.'

'Hand it over,' he says.

I do and silently pray that he doesn't notice how warm the phone is from being held for so long. But he says nothing and shuffles out the door and into the bedroom.

After turning off the light in the study, I head back out to check that the front and back door are locked, then I enter the bedroom to find Matt snoring again.

I glance at his bedside table.

For the first time since we've been married, his phone is nowhere to be seen.

24

'Let's go to the pub for dinner again,' Matt suggests, after an entire day of us hardly saying a word to each other. 'We haven't gotten around to trying the Monday special.'

I shrug. 'Okay. Anything has got to be better than sharing space with a moody husband.'

Neither of us have even attempted to discuss the trainwreck of an evening. Probably because we're both worried that it'll turn into another argument. And while I don't exactly want to sit at a table and look Matt in the eye right now – I don't even want to be near him, quite frankly – the idea of staying home alone with him is much worse. At least at the pub we'll be in the company of other people. Friendly faces. Which is what I need right now.

Honestly, I'm not even sure how I feel about yesterday. The random stranger banging on the door and leaving behind a note was one thing, but Matt hiding it from me, going as far as deleting the photo of it from my phone, and then acting like *I'd* done something wrong, was completely unfair.

Then there's the direct messages I found on his phone with MorningBird83. Although the conversations seemed innocent enough, I find it a little hurtful that he's been turning to this person more than he has to me, his own wife. And why was Jace mentioned? Unless someone in the group has the same name... that could be a possibility. But it just seems too coincidental.

I wait until Matt is showered and dressed and has left the room before I go in and get ready. I'm not really in the mood to dress up, but I force myself to make a bit of an effort. I grab a steely grey top and a pair of jeans from my wardrobe and finish the outfit with a green and orange scarf and a pair of comfy boots. My wavy hair is full of frizz, so I spritz it a little with some hair tamer spray.

Done.

The atmosphere between us in the car is frosty and I'm relieved when Matt pulls into a parking bay at the back of the pub. I get out immediately and take a deep lungful of the cool night air, as though I've been denied oxygen for the entire journey.

I follow Matt into the pub and relax as soon as we enter. There are people everywhere, lots of happy, smiling faces. A man is playing an acoustic guitar in the corner singing one of my favourite Bob Dylan songs, and a group of small kids are dancing in front of him.

We carefully navigate our way through the tables, cautious not to collide with the waiters ferrying plates to and fro. There are several lines of people at the bar waiting to order their food and drinks. The chicken parmigiana and spaghetti special is obviously a big drawcard on Monday evenings.

'Did you book a table?' I ask.

Matt nods and grimaces. 'I did.' He tries to hide his grin behind his wallet. 'I actually booked it this morning.'

I fold my arms across my chest and raise my brows. 'Oh, so you thought I was a sure thing, hey?'

We both look at each other and smile.

'Can we start fresh?' Matt asks. 'I hate this weird not-talking thing.'

'Me too.' I slip my arms around his waist. 'Can we be open with each other from now on? No more secrets?'

'No more secrets,' he says, bending to peck me on my forehead.

I exhale and nod towards the bar. 'Let's line up and order or else we'll be eating at midnight.'

He laughs and we join the queue. Twenty minutes later, we're seated at our reserved table and chatting away as though the events of the past twenty-four hours never happened.

'This is nice,' says Matt, his alcohol-free beer in his hand.

'It is,' I say, before taking a sip of my icy cold chardonnay. I lock eyes with Matt. 'Since we're not keeping secrets anymore, I want to discuss something. A couple of things, actually. And I want you to listen without reacting, at least until I'm finished speaking.'

Matt stiffens a little in his seat, and the crinkles around his eyes disappear, but he nods. 'Fair enough.'

I take another sip of wine. I'm going to need it.

'Okay. Firstly, I found the note that you tore up. And I put it back together like a jigsaw puzzle.'

Matt nods and rakes a hand through his hair, but he stays true to his word and doesn't say a word.

'Why did you tell me that it was nothing? The note literally said that someone wanted to hurt me. And then you went and deleted the photo of it from my phone. Don't you think I had a right to know about this?'

Matt thinks for a moment, then tears at the beer label before pressing it back against the glass.

'The man is obviously your stalker, and he knows a note like that would get your attention and have you calling.' Matt opens his palms. 'It's actually quite smart. If I hadn't torn it up, I bet you would have called him. Am I right?'

I grimace. 'I was actually going to call the number yesterday but George came along and I didn't get the chance.'

Matt sighs, whistling through his teeth. 'I'm sorry I went through your phone and deleted the photo. But I did it for your own good.'

A waiter delivers our order and sets the plates in front of us. We thank him and although the food smells delicious, we don't touch it yet.

'I suppose I should say that I'm sorry I went through your phone, too,' I say.

Matt meets my gaze. 'Did you find anything juicy?'

I contemplate mentioning the sheer number of messages between him and MorningBird83 but decide against it. Telling him about me borrowing George's car to go see Misha next weekend is more important. And I'm about to do so when George walks up and gives Matt a playful slap on the back.

Inwardly I groan. This is just my luck.

George looks at me and smiles. 'Amy's car is all ready for you. I've washed it, changed the oil, and filled the tank. The tyres are good too.' He looks at Matt and grins. 'Looks like you'll be eating here with me next weekend.'

Matt covers his surprise with a laugh and nods slowly while fixing me with a cold hard stare.

I'm not sure if George senses the sudden frosty air between us, but he waves at someone at the bar and says, 'Well, I'll let you two eat before your food gets cold. See you at the fair.' Then he leaves us to it.

'No more secrets, hey?' Matt asks.

'You won't believe me, but I was about to tell you just before George came up and said it.'

Matt sighs and picks up his knife and fork. 'Okay. I believe you. Now let's put this all behind us and enjoy this parmi that's bigger than our heads.'

'Deal,' I say, grinning. 'So what's this fair George mentioned?'

'Oh, it's something they do here for the kids on the school holidays.'

'Maybe we should go?'

'For sure,' says Matt, and we smile at each other.

Then we pick up our cutlery and tuck in.

An hour later, we're driving back home, our bellies full and the earlier frost between us well and truly thawed. Matt hasn't protested about me going away to visit with Misha. I'm not sure if it's because he's making a concerted effort to ease the tension between us and be more supportive of my right to make my own decisions, or if it's because he can't oppose it now that George has already prepared his wife's vehicle for me and would likely ask questions if I suddenly pulled out of the trip.

'I'm so full,' I grown, rubbing my belly as we turn onto our street.

'Maybe we can do something to burn it off,' Matt says, waggling his brows at me.

I laugh and shake my head at his audacity and then scream as Matt pulls into our driveway.

Matt slams on the brakes as a dark figure rushes towards the car. It's the same guy with the shaved head from last time and he's wearing a mask again.

I scream as he runs directly for my door, his eyes wide and zeroed in on me.

'Stay in the car and lock it once I get out,' Matt says, before he climbs out of his seat and yells at the guy to step away from the car and to get off our property.

I reach over and pull his door shut, then press the button that snaps all the locks shut.

The guy presses his palms against my window, his eyes wide, as he tries to tell me something. But Matt puts a hand over his mask-covered mouth and drags the man into the nearby bushes where there's no light, and I can no longer see them.

Although Matt has asked me to lock the doors and to keep them locked, I desperately want to help him. What if he's getting killed out there? But on the other hand, I'm also scared. Terrified of the masked man getting his hands on me.

For five long minutes I'm frozen with fear, unable to move. Then I can't stand to be alone any longer and unlock the car and get out.

'Matt?' I whisper into the night. All I can hear is the leaves of the large gum tree we have in our yard, rustling in the breeze. My scalp prickles and I shiver. 'Matt?' I hiss in the direction of the bushes.

I cry out as someone bursts out of the bushes, but cover my mouth when I see that it's Matt.

‘Oh my gosh, you scared the crap out of me. What happened? Where’s your jacket?’

Matt rests his hands on his knees and bends forward to catch his breath.

‘I lost it when we wrestled for a bit. But I chased him off. He’s gone into the forest.’ Once he’s caught his breath, Matt looks up at me. ‘He’s definitely your stalker. Did you see the way he ran to your car door? He could have had a knife. You could have gotten seriously hurt.’

‘Yeah,’ I say, my heart racing at the thought.

But I can’t help thinking about that note, and part of me wonders if that stranger was rushing to my door to warn me, not hurt me.

25

I wake up early to the comforting sound of rain pattering against the tin roof. Stalkers don't stalk in the rain, right?

Matt is sleeping soundly beside me, probably exhausted after chasing that stranger, and from being up for most of the night. I'd woken up past midnight to hear him coming in through the back door after we'd both gone to sleep. When I'd asked him what on earth he was doing outside in the dark, he said that he just needed to make sure that we were safe. That he couldn't sleep until he'd thoroughly checked our property. I told him that it was dangerous of him to do that alone. But he was already snoring beside me by the time I'd finished my sentence.

I slip out of bed quietly, wrapping my dressing gown around me, and leave the room with Swifty in my arms, closing the door behind me. In the kitchen I brew some coffee and pour some food into the cat bowl, then I draw open the curtains in the living room and settle on the couch to watch the rain.

With a blanket on my lap and a hot cup of coffee in my hand, I try to make sense of last night.

Who is that man and why was he limping towards me like that? He seemed so desperate to tell me something. And surely he wasn't planning to kidnap me or anything, not while knowing Matt was in the car with me. The more I think about it, the more I'm convinced that he was legitimately trying to warn me about something.

I check the time and am surprised that it's seven already. The rain clouds make it look like it's only dawn.

Matt's still asleep so I get up to make myself some breakfast. While I'm cracking eggs into a bowl, I hear the thump of the newspaper hitting the front door.

When his nan passed away, Matt forgot to cancel the newspaper delivery service, so we've kept it going. And I've gotten used to reading it over breakfast.

I unlock the front door and peer out across the driveway before stepping out.

The rain is only sprinkling now, and for some reason, the soft rushing sound the drops make as they hit the leaves on the trees and the tin roof, makes me feel safer.

Still, I need to be careful. That man could still be lurking around.

Matt went into the study and called the police last night. They said they'd send some officers to search the forest and surrounding areas as soon as they could, but we haven't heard back from them or seen any police around the property.

I make sure the coast is clear, then make a quick dash to retrieve the newspaper, which must have rolled over the edge of the veranda after it hit the door.

But after I pick it up and race back to the front door, I stop in my tracks.

There's a white envelope peeking out from beneath the door mat.

I pick it up. It's a little bit damp but the roof of the veranda has kept it mostly dry. I tuck it into my dressing gown pocket and head back inside, locking the door behind me.

'Morning,' says Matt, who's standing in the hallway, frowning. 'What were you doing outside? The police said to stay indoors until we get the all-clear.'

I wave the rolled newspaper. 'I was getting the paper.'

As I walk past him, I make sure that the envelope is buried deep in my pocket, then I place the newspaper on the counter.

Matt's already taking over the eggs I'd started, cracking in two more and adding chopped parsley and cream to the mix.

'Thanks,' I say. 'Want a cup tea?'

He nods and I turn on the kettle before heading to the toilet. Our kettle takes forever to boil and the noise will hopefully drown out the sound of me opening up the envelope.

Once I've locked the door behind me, I sit on the closed seat and take out the envelope. The dampness makes it a little less crinkly, which helps to minimise the noise.

With super-careful fingers, I take out the folded sheet of hotel note paper and open it up. It's from one of the beachside hotels in town. Whoever this man is, he's not a local.

The note is handwritten in black pen.

I read it over and over again, hot blood pounding in my ears.

> *Nadia,*
> *I wore a mask because I didn't want to frighten you.*
> *You know me, but not like I am now. The man you knew was a different person.*
> *Somebody did this to me. Someone that I love. They cut my brakes and tried to kill me.*
> *And now they're after you.*
> *I won't go into details in this letter, in case it gets into the wrong hands.*
> *But I need to speak with you.*
> *Call me on this number:*
> *0489 999 001*

I flush the toilet so as to create some noise, then I take out my phone and dial the number.

It goes straight to voicemail, but the recording confirms who I think it is.

Jace.

I try the number again and get the same result, Jace, asking the caller to leave a message.

So he didn't die in the accident.

But why isn't he answering his phone now that I'm finally calling him?

Who is he trying to warn me against?

The hairs on the back of my neck stand on end.

Maybe he didn't run off into the woods.

Maybe Matt did something to him.

I gasp with horror as it all clicks into place. The torn-up note. The fact that he put his hand over Jace's mouth while he was dragging him away from the car, so that Jace couldn't warn me.

Maybe Matt's the one who cut Jace's brakes. Maybe he's known all along about what happened in Busselton and has taken matters into his own hands.

My blood runs cold.

Jace may have been disfigured from the accident, but his wife died.

Which, if he is the one responsible, makes my husband a murderer.

26

'I'm heading out to fix some fences out the back,' says Matt, putting his breakfast dishes in the sink.

I couldn't eat a bite of the scrambled eggs after reading that letter. The thought of eating while Jace could by lying out there dead somewhere on our property, had turned my stomach.

'I'll be about an hour or so,' Matt continues. 'Promise me you'll stay inside. The police haven't gotten back to me yet.'

'But it's raining. Surely the fence work can wait,' I say, immediately suspicious of my husband's activities.

As if on cue, the drizzling rain grows heavy and begins to bucket down on the tin roof.

Matt glances out the window with a narrowed gaze, as though he's annoyed at the rain, but he turns back to me and shrugs. 'Work's got to be done, rain or shine.'

'I'll feel much safer if I come with you,' I say.

Matt shakes his head. 'No. You stay here.'

'Okay,' I say. But my heart is knocking against my chest. If Matt is so concerned for my welfare then he wouldn't leave my side today. The only plausible reason for him wanting to go out in that rain, by himself, is that he has something to get rid of.

Like a body.

I watch from the window as he goes into the shed and gets the tractor out, attaching a trailer behind it. While he drives it along the track at the side of the house, I notice that he has something green tucked under his arm. It's difficult to see through the heavy rain, but after I see a bit of it flapping around in the wind, I realise that he's carrying a tarpaulin.

I go to the front of the house and try to look through the peephole but I can't see a thing so I head into our bedroom and peer from behind the curtains.

My blood turns to ice. The tractor sits idling behind the bushes, the exact same bushes that he and Jace disappeared behind last night.

I put my hands to my mouth. This can't be happening. There can't be a body on our property. My husband could not have killed a man. He could not have killed Jace.

But then why didn't Jace answer his phone earlier?

And the letter. It all but confirms it.

Matt is the one that Jace was trying to warn me about.

My husband is a murderer.

Around five minutes later, I watch him drive the tractor back down the side of the property, noting that the tarpaulin is now covering something lumpy in the trailer.

All the blood drains from my head to my feet.

I make my way out of the room, feeling dizzy as I search for my phone. I eventually find it under Swifty, who's sleeping soundly on the couch, oblivious to all the chaos erupting around her.

I run for the study and google the local police station, then dial the number provided.

A woman answers the phone, asking me where she should direct my call.

'It's an emergency. Please, come out to 130 Parrot Bush Road,' I say, my eyes following Matt's movements through the window.

The tractor has now reached the edge of our acreage. He's already driven through the large back gate and is now heading along the boundary in the direction of the forest.

'What's the emergency exactly?' The woman asks.

'I think...' I swallow thickly. 'I think that someone has been murdered.'

The other end is silent for a few seconds, then the woman clears her throat.

'I'll send a couple of officers out right away. Let me get some details.'

I hang up before she can ask who I am. I know they'll be able to trace it back to me in the end. They have our address after all. I don't plan on lying to the officers either. But I do feel terribly guilty. As though I'm committing a crime against my husband, even though I know I'm doing the right thing.

Swifty enters the room and swirls around my legs, rubbing her head against me and purring. I pick her up and smother my face in her fur. I'm not sure how long I've been standing here at the window, lost in my thoughts, but it's long enough that I can't see Matt or the tractor anymore. He must have driven to the other side of the forest. Likely looking for a good place to bury the body.

A year ago, I would never have believed that Matt was capable of murder. But now... now I'm almost certain that he has.

Somebody bangs on the front door and I jump.

'Police!'

I run to the door and answer it.

'I made the call,' I say, my hands up. 'My husband has taken a tractor and a potential body out behind the forest.'

The female officer puts her phone to her lips. 'The forest. Now.' Then she shoves it in her pocket and regards me.

'I'm Constable Laci. May I come in?'

I nod and step aside to allow her to enter.

She sits down at the dining table while I head into the kitchen and pop the kettle on.

'Would you like tea or coffee? Or a glass of water?' I ask.

'Take a seat please... Ah... your name?'

'Nadia. Nadia Freeman. My husband is Matthew.'

She taps this information into her phone.

'Why do you think your husband is trying to bury a body?'

I take a deep breath and it all spills out. The stalker back home, then the man with the shaved head showing up with the note. Then the letter, which turned out to be from Jace, my former boss, who is now suspiciously missing after Matt wrested him into the bushes last night.

'But why would your husband cut the brakes of your former boss? And then kill him?'

'My husband gets easily jealous... He calls it being protective. And he may have discovered something secret that happened between Jace and me one weekend.'

'Discovered what exactly?'

'That I slept with Jace. It was a one-time thing,' I add, as though that makes it less immoral.

Constable Laci's expression doesn't change, but she does tap more notes in her phone.

'And tell me, how do you think he found out about this secret affair?'

'It wasn't an affair,' I say. I think about her question and shake my head. 'I'm not really sure, but...'

I think about the video. Maybe he came across it on a porn site. Maybe a friend recognised me from behind the mask and sent it to him. The thought horrifies me. I decide not to tell the officer about the video, or the money that I received for it.

'Is your husband ever violent with you? Has he ever been abusive?'

I shake my head. 'No. Not at all.'

Constable Laci's phone rings and she gets up to answer it, moving into the living room to take a peek out the window. 'Okay. Roger that.'

She puts the phone away into her pocket. 'We're done here. It was a false alarm.'

'False alarm?' I stand. 'Did the officers find my husband?'

'They did. It seems he had a pile of fence longs and coils of wire under that tarp, not a body like you thought.'

'But what about the letter? It said that someone was trying to hurt me.'

'We'll look into it.' She raises her brows. 'May I take it with me back to the station? We'll see if we can locate this former boss of yours and make sure that he is okay.'

I nod and pluck the letter from the table and hand it to her. In exchange, she gives me a card with her name and number on it.

'I'll be in touch,' she says, and sees herself out the front door.

I watch, through the screen door, as the officers pile back into their police vehicles and drive away.

Then I hear the rattly sound of the tractor retuning and race to the living room window in time to see Matt reversing it, along with the trailer, into the shed.

Although the rain has eased off for now, Matt looks soaked to the bone. I can't see the expression on his face from this far away, but I can tell by the stiffness in his gait that he's not happy.

27

'The police?' Matt says, when he steps inside into the laundry and lays eyes on me. His clothes are dripping mud and water all over the tiles and onto a cat statue that I use as a doorstop.

'I can't believe that you think I could murder someone! How do you think I feel knowing that my own wife thinks I'm capable of murderer?' He shakes his head and pushes past me. 'I'm going to take a shower.'

'Wait,' I say. 'Did you know that the stranger who's been coming around is Jace? My old boss? Did the police tell you?'

Matt's eyes widen slightly, and his mouth twitches, but he looks away and tries to act as though the name means nothing to him.

'No,' he says, 'why?'

His mouth twitches again. I know that he's lying.

'How do you know?' he asks sharply. 'Have you been talking to him?'

There's a menace to my husband's voice that I don't like.

'I just know,' I say, deciding not to mention the letter.

Matt mutters something under his breath.

'What was that?' I ask.

'Nothing,' he says. 'I need a shower. I'm freezing.'

I watch him disappear down the hallway.

A minute later the pipes begin to rattle through the walls and I know that I don't have much time.

I don't bother packing any clothes. Misha is the same size as me and I'm sure she'll be happy to loan me some of her clothes as soon as I get to Albany, so I just take the essentials with me. Some food for Swifty and my phone and handbag. Swifty happily hops into her carrier after I pop some treats inside of it.

The shower is still running when I carry Swifty out the front door. Once I'm past the driveway, I make a dash for George's place.

The rain has stopped, thank God. But my sneakers are a muddy mess and soaked through by the time I make it to my neighbour's place.

George opens the door before I get a chance to knock on it.

'I saw the cops leave and then I saw you running over. What's wrong, love? Is Matthew alright?'

'I need to borrow Amy's car today. Please, George. Right now. I can't explain but I might be in danger.'

George's eyes fly open. 'Okay, love, okay.'

Swifty meows from inside the carrier.

'Oh, you have Maida's cat with you... this is serious then.' He ushers me inside and glances around behind me before closing the door.

'Is he hurting you?'

I shake my head. 'Not really. I wish I had time to explain it all, but I think I'm in danger and I need to leave right now because it's not safe for me to stay.'

'Then that's all I need to know.' He plucks some keys from a wooden hook rack on the wall. 'Here,' he says, handing me a key with a pumpkin keyring dangling from it. He notices me staring at it.

'I used to call Amy my pumpkin.' He half smiles, then his expression grows serious. 'Okay. Let's get you going.' As he walks me out the back door and towards the shed, he looks around as though waiting for Matt to come charging from out of the bushes. But thankfully he doesn't.

'Luckily, I warmed her up this morning. I've been starting it up every day since you asked about it. So it's all ready to go. The tank's full too. Where did you say you were going?'

'Albany.'

'It'll get you there without stopping.' George taps his nose. 'But if Matthew asks, you're heading into the city.'

I breathe a sigh of relief and feel a rush of gratitude for this kind man.

'Thank you so much, George. Can I get your phone number please?' He gives me a landline and I save it in my phone. 'I'll call you once I get there.'

I load Swifty into the back seat, strapping her carrier in using the seat belt, then close the door.

'You're amazing, George,' I say, hand over heart. 'And please take care of yourself. Is Annette back yet?'

He shakes his head. 'I think some relative of hers is in trouble. I'm not sure when she'll be back.'

'Maybe you should go into town today and visit a friend,' I say. 'I'm not sure that it's safe around here. I'd hate to leave you out here all alone.'

George waves off my concern. 'I'm a tough old bloke. I'll be okay. You get going, don't worry about me.'

'Thank you.'

I get into the driver's seat and adjust it forward a little. Then I put the key in the ignition and fire up the engine. It purrs nicely. I give George a big thumbs up and travel along the gravel driveway and out onto the road.

My heart stops when I see a figure walking along the road behind me in my rearview mirror. When I recognise the green and black chequered shirt, my pulse quickens.

It's Matt and he's walking with his head down. But once he hears the car take off, he looks up and starts to run towards me.

I put my foot down and drive as fast as I can, until he disappears from view.

28

Once Matt disappears from view, I slow down, putting my foot on the brake pedal. It feels a little spongy, but I guess that's to be expected with such an old car. I'll have to remember to drive extra carefully on the journey though.

I slow the car down as I turn onto the highway and I can't help but notice a black car with tinted windows parked on the side of the road. Someone is sitting inside of it with their head down, as though they're trying not to be seen. I get the feeling it's a woman. But I can't be sure because the windows are so dark.

I grip my steering wheel and turn my attentions to the road ahead of me. Even though I want to get as far away from Matt as possible, I can't risk having an accident along the way. I make a point to stick to the speed limit, hoping that George has stuck to his plan of telling Matt that I'd headed in the opposite direction.

Once the town is far behind me and no cars are trailing me, I pull into a parking bay, noticing once again how spongy my brakes are, which sets me on edge after knowing that Jace's brakes had been cut the night his wife died.

But this is George's wife's car, and it's been sitting in a garage since she died, under his watchful eye. It's more likely that the brakes are old and need new pads.

Once the car finally rolls to a halt, behind a parked truck, I take out my phone and dial up Misha, then put it on speaker.

She answers almost immediately. 'You'd better not be calling to say that you're not coming this weekend.'

'Don't worry, I'm coming,' I say. 'Right now.'

'What? What do you mean?'

The truck starts up and I turn the phone off speaker and put it to my ear instead.

'What's that?' she asks. 'Where are you?'

'It's a truck. I'm in a parking bay.'

'What the hell? Is everything okay?'

'I'll explain when I get to your place. But I'm coming now.'

'As in, *now*, now?'

An engine revs behind me and my heart contracts when I see a flashy red sports car, with even darker windows than the black car, pull up beside me.

'Shit. I've got to go.'

'Nadia?'

I end the call and start the car and immediately put it into drive before slamming my foot on the accelerator.

Once I turn onto the highway, the car follows me, and when I increase my speed, the red car matches it, which sends my heart rate skyrocketing. The truck from the parking bay comes into view up ahead and a sign informs me that an overtaking lane will be opening up in five hundred metres.

This may be my only chance to lose the driver tailing me.

As soon as the extra lane opens up, I put my foot down. The engine groans as I put it under way too much pressure for an engine that's been resting, but it eventually gets me past the truck and soon I'm flying back into the inside lane.

Up ahead, another parking bay comes into view, which is perfect timing. I plan on slowing down and pulling into the bay just as the mystery person following me overtakes the truck and zooms ahead. Then I'll have time to turn back around and head back into town to the police station.

Swifty begins to meow from the back seat.

'It's okay, girl,' I say, trying my best to soothe her.

I gently ease my foot down onto the brake pedal so that I can pull into the parking bay, but instead of the sponginess I'm expecting, the action creates a hissing sound and the pedal goes straight down to the floor. Much to my horror, I keep barrelling forward.

The next thing I know the red car overtakes the truck and moves ahead of me, which is a problem, because the overtaking lane has closed, so I have nowhere else to go.

'It's okay, sweetie,' I tell Swifty, who I know is frightened by the way that she's meowing.

I keep pressing my foot against the brake pedal but of course the car won't slow down.

The driver of the red car suddenly slams on their brakes, and because another vehicle towing a caravan is coming the other way, I'm forced to turn my speeding car off-road onto the gravel. And although I manage to keep the car straight for several hundred metres, when the truck finally whooshes past me, I'm spooked and end up turning the car straight into the bush. But after skidding over shrubs and narrowly missing thick tree trunks, I finally come to a halt in front of a fallen log, dust flying into the car.

I sit in shock for a few seconds before I realise that the red car has pulled up on the side of the road about a hundred metres away. There's no way I'll get my car out of these bushes, so as quickly as I can I get out of the car and open the back door to take Swifty out.

But as soon as I do, somebody comes from behind me and rips the carrier out of my hands.

I scream and give chase to the blond man, who is wearing a black cap, and sunglasses, but he can move faster than me and once he's a few metres away, he opens the carrier and dumps Swifty onto the ground.

'No!' I watch helplessly as my terrified cat, her fur puffed with fear, runs deep into the bushes. I scream at the man. 'How could you do that to an innocent animal?'

He turns his attentions to me and I note that he's clean shaven and dressed in slacks and a dress shirt. I've never seen him in my life.

'What do you want from me?' I ask, taking a small side step in the direction of the road. If I manage to run fast enough, I might make it out of this bush and onto the highway where I can wave somebody down for help.

The man walks slowly towards me, his face red.

'Payback,' he says.

'For what? I don't even know you,' I say, taking another step towards the road.

'You hurt my sister,' he says.

'Your sister? How when I don't even know who you're talking about.'

'Of course you do.'

I shake my head and shuffle towards the road.

'Did you cut my brakes?' I ask. 'Are you the one who cut Jace's brakes as well?'

The man chuckles and I feel sick to my stomach. I'd accused my own husband when it was somebody else, a stranger, all along that had killed Jace's wife. Matt had only been trying to keep me safe. Just like Jace had done his best to protect me.

'Jace tried to warn me about you.'

The man shrugs and moves closer.

'Well, the dead can't talk, so he won't be warning you anymore.'

Oh my god. This man killed Jace. Bile rises up in my throat. I take another step towards the road.

He takes two more towards me.

'I know you very well, Nadia.' He grins, revealing pointed teeth. 'Very, very well. I've watched your video.'

I freeze, my stomach churning sickly.

'Now, let's get this over and done with. If you don't run, I'll make it painless and quick. But if you run and I catch you, you're going to suffer. And I might have a little fun with you before you die.'

I bolt, praying that Swifty uses her feline senses to run as far away from this evil man as possible and get herself home safely. I tear through the bushes, sharp branches digging into my skin until my sneakers hit gravel and I run along the side of the highway.

The man is fast, closing the distance between us quickly.

I start to wave my hands around in the air, desperately trying to catch the attention of an approaching car, and I gasp with relief when I hear a driver shift gears and slow their car down.

The footsteps behind taper off and I reduce speed, risking a glance over my shoulder. The man's no longer chasing me, but is instead making a run for his car.

The Landcruiser comes to a halt, sending a storm of gravel flying all over the shiny red car. The driver gets out. A man with thick white hair who looks to be in his late seventies. By the time he makes his way over to me, my attacker hops into the red car and gets away, making a U-turn and heading back towards Saltbush Bay.

'Are you okay?' the man asks.

I nod, then think about Swifty and release a sob.

'He ran me down. My car's in the bush... then he threw my cat out of her carrier and chased me. He was going to kill me.'

The man looks like he's about to have a heart attack. His skin has turned pale and his hands are shaking. 'Let's get you into the car. I'll drive you to the nearest police station.'

'Thank you,' I say.

But as I'm about to get into the Landcruiser, Matt pulls up in front of it and gets out, rushing to my side.

'Misha called me. She was hysterical. Are you okay?' He eyes the man with suspicion.

'This kind man stopped to help me,' I say.

The gentleman nods, looking even paler than before.

'Is everything okay?' the man asks.

'Yes. This is my husband, Matthew,' I say, smiling at the man to demonstrate that I'm okay.

'I'll take care of her from here,' Matt says. 'Thank you, sir.'

The man nods and climbs back into his car. He gets his phone out and takes a photo of Matthew's car, then drives away.

'Thank God you're safe,' says Matt, wrapping his arms around me. I sink into his embrace and sob with relief but then I remember Swifty.

'Swifty! He threw her out of the carrier.'

Matt doesn't even ask me why I had taken Swifty and why I'd taken off like that, but immediately begins helping me to search through the bushes for our beloved cat.

When I spot the carrier I run over to it, and to my surprise, see a patch of grey fur poking through the netting. I peer inside and find Swifty backed into the corner, her eyes dark and wild.

'It's okay, sweetie. It's okay. We're going to take you home now.' I stroke her soft fur to sooth her and she begins to purr immediately, then I zip up the carrier.

'Thank God,' Matt says and sighs with relief. He puts his arms around me and kisses my forehead. 'Thank God you're both okay.'

'I can't believe she got back into her carrier,' I say, gazing down at her through the mesh top. 'What a clever girl you are.'

We make our way back to Matt's car, my heart pounding anxiously all the while. I wait for the red car to come barrelling down the road towards me. But it doesn't.

'Can we go straight home?' I ask. 'I'll call the police from there. I think it'll be too much for Swifty to go down to the station after what she's been through.'

'Anything you want. Let's get you girls home,' Matt says.

'Poor Swifty will be so relieved to get back home. Me too,' I say. Then I look over at Matt as he starts the car and puts it into gear. 'I'm sorry for taking off like that. I've just been so confused lately.'

Matt puts a hand up. 'Leave it for now. Let's get you home safe. It can wait. I just want my girls safe.'

I smile and settle into the seat, running my fingers across the strands of fur poking out of the carrier and Swifty purrs.

I may not know who that man is, and why he's trying to kill me.

But at least I'm safe with Matt.

29

Swifty is clingy when we get home, and refuses to leave my side, so I make myself a cup of tea with her perched on my shoulder like a parrot.

'You probably should go to the police station. That man could have killed you,' Matt says, gnawing on his bottom lip. He looks nervous, his eyes darting all over the place as he leans against the kitchen bench and watches me make my tea.

'I'm going to call them as soon as I finish making this tea.'

'I'd feel better if you went to the station. The man's dangerous.'

I get the milk out of the fridge and pour some into my tea.

'Leave it out,' says Matt

'You sound like you know this man?'

Matt sighs wearily and rubs his face. 'How on earth would I know this person?'

'Well for starters you talk to a bunch of people online, telling them God knows what.' It comes out like an accusation, which I didn't intend.

'Oh gee, thanks. So it's all my fault, is it?' He storms out the kitchen.

'I didn't mean it like that,' I call after him.

Swifty trills and shifts around on my shoulder, trying to make herself more comfortable. I take her, along with my mug of tea, into the study.

While I'm sitting at the desk with my phone to my ear, on hold for Constable Laci, there's a light knock on the open study door. I swivel in my seat.

'George is here,' Matt says, widening his eyes and grimacing. 'I'll tell him what happened and explain about his wife's car. Then I suppose I'll arrange for a tow.'

'Please tell him how sorry I am. I'll get it fixed and pay for everything. And ask him to wait if you can, because I need to explain something to him.'

'No worries,' Matt says, and I give him the thumbs up just as Constable Laci answers.

'Hi, it's Nadia Freeman. I need to report something.'

'Is it your husband again?'

'No. I got that completely wrong. But somebody *is* trying to hurt me and I have reason to believe that this same man is responsible for a woman's death in a car accident earlier this year. He also implied that he killed Jace Green, my former boss.'

'Do you know this man's name?'

'No. All I know is that he tried to run me off the road this afternoon. I crashed the car I was driving and he chased me through the bushes. If it wasn't for a kind stranger who stopped to help me, I'd probably be dead by now.'

'Okay. I'm going to need some details,' Constable Laci says. The evenness of her tone and the calmness in her voice sets me at ease. 'Can you start by giving me a description of your attacker?'

I describe every detail I can remember, the pointy teeth, the small bits of blond hair peeking out from his cap. Then I describe his car, recalling the first half of his licence plate.

'Okay. That's good,' she says. 'Leave it with me for now. Go get some rest and we'll be in touch shortly.'

'Will you let me know if you find him?' I ask.

'We'll need you to come into the station at some stage, to give an official statement, likely tomorrow, so we might have some news for you by then. But for now, stay home and get some rest. I'll call you within the next twenty-four hours. Keep your doors and windows locked and call me if you see or hear from him again.'

'Will do. Thank you, Constable Laci.'

She hangs up.

Matt appears at the study door, frowning and looking unsettled. 'George is waiting to see you. He's being weird with me.'

'Oh,' I say, grimacing. 'That's my fault. I may have said some things earlier to cause him to believe that you were a threat to me.'

'Bloody hell, Nards. Why would you do that?'

'Because... you've been acting strangely.'

'You're the one who's been acting weird,' he fires back. 'Accusing me of things I didn't do.'

At the angry tone of Matt's voice, Swifty springs up from my lap and dashes out of the room.

'I know. And I'm sorry. But it's been a confusing couple of days. Let me explain everything to George. He'll understand.'

I get up and brush past Matt who stiffens at my touch.

'Nadia,' says George, his eyes shifting between Matt and me. 'Are you okay? Tell me the truth because I can't make sense of anything.'

It's going to be extra difficult to convince George that everything is fine between Matt and me when the air between us is so hostile right now.

'Sorry, George,' I say, sighing. 'I know this must seem confusing. I did initially think that Matt was trying to hurt me, but I got it wrong. It was a stranger all along. Some man in a red sports car tried to run me off the road today. He's dangerous and he may have already killed others.'

'That bastard,' says George. 'Do you know him?'

'No. And I don't know why he's after me, but we all need to be extra careful.' I glance at Matt and offer a soft smile. 'But it's not Matt we need to worry about. So you don't have to worry, George. I'm safe here.'

'As long as you're sure,' says George, still eying Matt with suspicion.

I try to give a reassuring smile. 'I'm absolutely sure.'

'Okay then. I believe you.' He leans in to give me a brief hug and whispers in my ear. 'You have my number just in case.'

When he pulls away, I nod and mouth a thank you.

George seems satisfied and lets Matt see him out. As they disappear out the front door, a sudden wave of exhaustion hits me like a truck. I plonk myself down on the couch beside Swifty and rest my head against the top of the couch.

'Are you okay?' Matt asks when he returns. 'Are you hungry? I can make you something if you are.'

'No. I'm not hungry. But thank you.' I can't stop thinking about what happened today. I think I'm still in shock. One minute I'm driving down to Misha's, the next someone is trying to kill me. 'I actually should ring Misha. She's got to be worried.'

'No need. I called her already and filled her in because I knew she would be stressing about you. She said she's glad you're safe and that she'll call you in the morning.' He comes to stand behind the couch and strokes my forehead. 'Now. Let me at least make you a snack. How about toast?'

'Okay then. With apricot jam, please.'

He smiles and disappears into the kitchen.

While he's gone, his phone, which is resting on the coffee table, lights up and I lean forward to take a peek at it.

It's a private message notification from MorningBird83 and it simply says,

My brother is missing.

I'm taken aback. Not because this woman's brother is missing. But the fact she has reached out to my husband. Turned to him at her time of need. There's something so intimate about that single sentence. You don't just blurt out such serious news, with no context, unless you know the other person extremely well.

I stoke Swifty's fur and wonder who MorningBird83's brother is. And what's happened to him.

Matt returns with a steaming mug of tea and a plate with two slices of apricot jam toast cut into rectangles.

'Thanks,' I say. 'I think I left my other tea in the study.'

'I know. It was cold so I tipped it out.'

'You got a message.' I nod toward his phone and he immediately picks it up. He stares at the screen for several seconds, then blinks, before he shoves the phone in his pocket.

'Is everything okay?' I ask.

'It's nothing.'

'Really?'

He looks at me and I think it's dawned on him that I read the notification.

'My friend has a younger brother that's always getting himself into trouble. And now he's missing.'

A few minutes later, he sits down beside me with his own plate of toast, looking completely unbothered that one of his close AA friends has a missing brother. 'Should we find a movie on telly?'

'Yeah. Sure,' I say.

Matt gets up to draw the curtains closed then finds a station showing *Jurassic Park* and we settle in to watch it. But I find it difficult to keep my mind on the film.

I can't stop wondering if Matt has been having an affair, and if this is the reason why he has been so protective of me. Because he doesn't want me finding out.

'Who is it that wrote to you? This MorningBird83?'

'Huh?' Matt keeps his eyes fixed on the screen.

'Is it a man or a woman?'

'It's no one important,' he says. 'Don't worry about it.' He gets up. 'I'm still hungry. You want an omelette? I'm going to make myself one.'

'No. Thanks. The toast was enough.'

Ten minutes later, he sits back down on the couch with his omelette, again, seemingly unbothered. Swifty hops off my lap to go and sniff at his plate. Then she decides she'd rather her own food and trots off to her bowl.

I get up to feed her, emptying one of her favourite sachets into her bowl, when a newsflash interrupts the movie.

A body has been found. Male. In his thirties.

My blood pounds loudly in my ears, then my heart takes a dive.

Jace.

They must have found him.

I throw the empty sachet in the bin and wash my hands at the sink and in the reflection of the window, see Matt disappear down the hallway in the direction of the study. He's probably calling MorningBird83. But why would he do that immediately after he saw the report about the dead man? Does he think that the body belongs to MorningBird83's missing brother?

I have a strong feeling in my gut that I'm missing something.

It's all too coincidental. There must be a link somewhere between all the strange things that have been happening lately. But I just haven't got enough dots to connect yet.

Matt returns to the living room and plonks himself down on the couch, then yawns.

'You sound tired,' I say.

He blinks at me, the whites of his eyes red and gritty-looking. 'I am. I think I need an early night.'

'Really? But it's only seven-thirty.'

'I didn't really sleep well last night.'

I think about how I caught him coming back into the house in the middle of the night.

'Were you talking to someone just now in the study?'

'Nah. I was just doing a search on that story that flashed on the news. I wanted to see if they'd identified the body.'

'Oh. Okay. Were you thinking that it was someone in particular?'

'I was just curious.' He rubs his face and blinks. 'I seriously need some sleep. Sorry, Nards. Let's talk in the morning. Oh, and that fair is on in town tomorrow. The Saltbush Bay Show. George reminded me when I walked him out. He also said that there'll be stalls there, for locals to sell things. You should bring some of your biscuits. Everyone will love 'em. But I can understand if you don't want to after what you went through today.'

I picture spending tomorrow cooped up in the house with Matt hovering over me. No. That's the last thing I need. I want to be around people. Normal people. And what could be safer than being in a public place filled with families and kids, the entire Saltbush Bay community?

'I do actually have a whole heap of biscuits. I only baked them yesterday.'

'Great. So we'll go then.' He leans over to kiss me. 'Maybe tomorrow we can actually forget about all of this and have some fun. Put it behind us.'

I think about Constable Laci and how she mentioned that they'll want me to come into the station to make a statement tomorrow. But I don't bother telling Matt. He needs some shut eye and today would have been almost as stressful for him as it was for me.

'Goodnight,' I say, as he shuffles down the hallway towards our bedroom.

Matt and I are so different. Where he gets sleepy after a stressful event, I go the opposite way and become hyper alert. Even though I feel exhausted physically, there's no way I could go to sleep right now the way my brain is ticking. Instead I take out my biscuit containers and a box of jars that Maida had kept in her spare room, and I set about sterilising them in the oven. Once they're cool, I fill them with my baked goods, then make pretty labels for them and tie pale pink ribbons around them all.

By the time I'm finished, it's past midnight, and my eyelids have finally grown heavy. I brush my teeth and get into my pyjamas, then, just as I'm getting into bed, Matt's phone lights up.

He's snoring and doesn't flinch at the light, so I tiptoe over to read the notification.

It's from MorningBird83 and it says,

> *If it was you, I'll never speak to you again.*

30

The next day, Matt is notably distant, his mind off somewhere else, and I'm sure it's got something to do with the message he received from MorningBird83.

'Do you still want to go to the fair?' I ask. Although I'm itching to get out of the house and be around the townspeople, I also can't help but remember Constable Laci's advice to stay home and keep the doors and windows locked until I hear from her.

Matt's been parked on the couch since he woke up, staring out through the living room window in the direction of the forest. He looks at me and blinks, then eyes all the jars I packed into boxes last night, sitting on the counter.

'May as well,' he says. 'What else are we going to do with all those biscuits?'

He gets up and helps me load all the biscuit jars into the back of the car and we head out to the fair as planned.

When we arrive at the park in town, it's already buzzing with activity, which makes it difficult to find a parking spot. The fair hasn't even started yet. But eventually Matt mounts a curb and parks beneath a tree on the side of the road.

'What a beautiful day,' I say to Matt, once we're out of the car.

The sun is out and dragonflies soar through the air across the grass. You wouldn't know that it had been pouring with rain yesterday.

'You can choose any of these tables,' a woman named June tells us.

Matt picks one towards the left, conveniently located beside the sausage sizzle station. I lay a red and white chequered tablecloth down and arrange the biscuit jars so that they are in groups by type. Macadamia and white-choc chip, Anzac biscuits, pecan dainties and Matt's favourite, my cornflake cookies.

'These look great,' says June, coming over with a small white board for our table. 'You can write your prices on this.'

'Thanks. Is there a fee?' I ask and June waves me away and almost looks cross that I suggested it. 'We're a *community* here.' Then she moves across to the next table, where a woman is carefully laying down crocheted items.

'You want something from that table, don't you,' says Matt, seeming more himself.

I smile. 'Maybe if I make some money, I'll spend it all here. Put it back into *the community*.'

He laughs. 'I'm going to go for a walk and see what else is for sale. I'll report back soon.'

I look around and spy George talking to a group of men who are all standing around various woodwork projects. They must be his friends from the Men's Shed group. He sees me and waves. I wave back.

People are beginning to trickle in and gather around the stalls and suddenly I'm surrounded by customers thrusting cash and coins my way, telling me which biscuits they'd like.

I glance around for Matt and sigh with relief when I see him jogging back towards our table.

'Sorry. I may or may not have gotten asked to sample some jam donuts,' he says, sugar crystals coating his lips. He brushes them off and rubs his hands together. 'What do you want me to do?'

'Get the extras from under the table and arrange them into groups. We're going to sell out I think.'

We soon settle into a happy rhythm with Matt handing over the jars and me collecting the money and giving change.

'I'll take three jars of the macadamia and white-choc chip,' says a man with two children dangling from his arms and twisting at his wrists like little monkeys.

'Great choice,' I say, then I notice, from out the corner of my eye, Matt escorting a tall, thin lady away from the table. She is wearing a silk scarf wrapped over her head and looks extremely pale. I can't think why Matt would be steering a customer away from my stall but then I get a glimpse of her face and freeze.

It's Dawn. Jace's sister.

But she looks so different to how she appeared the last time I saw her. She has lost a lot of weight and is obviously very ill. But it's her.

'I said, do you have change for a fifty? Hello?'

I blink and turn back to the man.

'I'm so sorry. Yes. I do have the change.' My mind is a scramble and I think I give the man back more than I need to, but I can't think straight.

'Thanks,' the man says, and hands his children a jar each and keeps one for himself. 'Can I eat mine now?' the girls asks as they walk away.

'I'd like a jar of the Anzac's please,' asks an elderly man with a kind smile. 'My wife used to make them and I miss her so much.'

I'm touched and place a jar into his hands and wave away his five-dollar note.

A woman asks for two jars of pecan dainties and while I pass her the change for her twenty dollars, I can't keep my eyes off Matt, who now looks like he is engaged in a heated argument with Dawn.

Then it hits me like a slap to the face. I'm almost dizzy with the realisation and need to pause for a moment to take it in.

The teenage boy standing in front of me frowns and decides he doesn't want my biscuits after all.

Dawn is MorningBird83.

And her missing brother is *Jace*.

And judging by the message that lit up his phone on his bedside last night, she thinks that Matt has something to do with his disappearance.

Dawn marches towards my table while Matt calls after her.

'Excuse me for a moment,' I say to the now-very-confused customers who are still waiting.

'Nadia. I need to speak with you. Alone,' Dawn says. 'It's about Jace and it's important.'

Matt comes to her side. 'It's time to leave,' he says, through gritted teeth.

Dawn reaches out and slips something into my hand. I wrap my fingers around it, and when Matt isn't looking, I take a quick peek at it. It's a pen, from the same hotel Jace was stayed at when he wrote me that letter.

Dawn and I lock eyes and I nod. Then she tugs herself free from Matt's grasp and walks away.

I shove the pen in my pocket.

'What was that she gave you?' Matt asks.

'A pen. Help me serve the remaining customers, please,' I say, before smiling at the two kids who are next in line.

Matt begrudgingly begins handing out jars and I worry that his forced clownish smile is going to scare the customers away. But I'm too busy thinking about Dawn and the fact that she and my husband have been speaking online for nearly a year, to say anything.

When we watch the last jar of biscuits get carried away, he turns to me.

'Give me a look at that pen.'

'No,' I say, pulling away from him.

Matt opens his mouth to speak but stops and stares at something behind me, his shoulders sinking as he sighs as though in defeat.

I turn and see Constable Laci accompanied by a young, male officer.

'This is Constable Small,' she says, her expression grim. 'We'd like you both to join us at the station for questioning.'

31

'What's this about?' Matt asks.

Some of the people gathered at the nearby stalls stop what they're doing to watch us. I can imagine that by tonight, when the news spreads that the police have taken us in for questioning, we'll be the talk of the town. The new folk. The grandson of Maida Freeman and his wife attracting murderers and bringing dead bodies to the community.

'Come with us and we can explain everything at the station,' Constable Laci says calmly.

'Should we come in our own car?' I ask.

'We'll drive you there. It's close, so you can walk back to get your car afterwards.'

I look at Matt and he shrugs. 'Okay, I guess.'

After a short drive, where none of us speak, we arrive at the station and are split into separate interview rooms. Constable Laci stays with me, but Constable Small takes Matt into another room. After she sets a recording device on the table, turning it on to record, she states my name and makes a note of the date and time.

'Okay,' she says. 'So I'm going to ask you to file a report on the man who ran you off the road yesterday. We have managed to identify him based on the information you provided.' She sighs. 'However, we can't locate him. He dumped his vehicle in Mandurah.'

I take this in. The man who tried to kill me is still on the loose. But at least he is in Mandurah and not in

Saltbush Bay anymore. I still want him caught as soon as possible.

'What's his name? And do you think he had something to do with the body you found?'

'Chad Burrows is the name of your attacker. Is it a name you're familiar with?'

I say the name aloud but shake my head.

'Okay. Well, as for the murder victim, we're just trying to gain as much information as possible.' She inhales deeply and slides a photo across to me. 'The victim whose body was discovered yesterday has been identified by his sister.'

My blood runs cold when I see the man's face. Without the medical mask, I can see just how much damage the car accident had done to his handsome face. A long, thick, pearly pink jagged scar runs from his left cheek, through his nose and across the corner of his mouth.

Constable Laci watches me carefully.

'It's Jace,' I say, my voice hoarse.

'Your former employer, am I correct?'

'How did he die?' I ask, shivering at the lifelessness in Jace's eyes.

Constable Laci clears her throat and I meet her gaze. 'His neck was broken. His body dumped at the local rubbish tip.'

I gasp and bring a hand to my mouth. Poor Jace.

'You need to find that man who attacked me. He's responsible for murdering Jace. He implied that he knew he was dead already.'

Constable Laci nods. 'That's what we're trying to do.' She clears her throat and clasps her hands together on the table. 'You said yesterday that Jace had been at your house two nights ago, distressed and rushing at your car. Do you have any idea why?'

I glance at the picture again and shudder.

'He was warning me about someone wanting to hurt me. But I never got to find out who or why because Matt, my husband, dragged him away into the bushes.'

Constable Laci nods and turns off the recording device.

'Okay. I'll go get the paperwork for you to sign and then you are free to go.'

'Will Matt be released too?'

'I can't say. I'll check in on him now and let you know.' She stands. 'I'll be back in a moment.'

Once she returns, I fill out the paperwork and sign it before sliding it back across the table.

'You're free to go,' she says. 'But don't leave town.'

'Does this mean I'm a suspect in Jace's murder?'

'No. It means your life might be in danger. That man tried to kill you once. He might try again. Stay home. Lock your windows and doors and we'll be in touch.'

I get up and thank her.

'Nadia?' she says, as I'm on my way out of the room.

'Yes?'

'Your husband will be staying at the station for a little while longer so I suggest you go straight home. It could be a long night.' She tosses me the keys to the car.

'Is he under arrest?' I ask.

'No. He's just helping us with our investigation at this point.'

I nod and walk out of the station, feeling strange, like I'm floating in a dream. No, not a dream – a nightmare.

I walk back to the car, with every intention to head straight home like Constable Laci advised, but when I get into the driver's seat, something sharp digs into my legs and I remember Dawn and her pen. So instead of heading home I drive straight to the hotel she's staying at, and park in one of the guest parking bays.

The sea breeze is cool and blows right through my clothes, but it's refreshing and clears my head. Gulls squawk in the distance as they circle a family eating fish and chips on a patch of lawn beside a playground.

Once inside, I ask at the reception desk for Dawn. But of course they refuse to give any information away. Luckily, I spot her sitting at a table in the lobby bar, a cup of tea in front of her.

'Nadia,' she says, waving me over.

'Dawn,' I say, her brother's morgue photo fresh in my mind. 'I'm so sorry to hear about Jace.'

She closes her eyes briefly and nods. 'Please join me,' she says, and I take a seat opposite her. 'I've been waiting for you.' Dawn clears her throat and takes a sip of her tea.

I note how slender her arms are now, and the pencilled-in eyebrows. She must be going through a rough time with her health and now she has to grieve her brother through all of this.

She regards me across the table. 'Tell me something, please. And tell me the truth.'

'Of course,' I say, looking her directly in the eye. 'You can ask me anything.'

'Was Jace at your house two nights ago?'

'Yes he was,' I say.

Dawn sets the teacup down onto its saucer, her hands trembling.

'Why would Matthew lie to me about that? Jace told me he was going to your house, to warn you. To tell you that you were in danger.' Her thin, bony hands clench into fists. 'But when I messaged Matthew last night and asked him if he'd seen Jace, he told me he hadn't.'

'I don't know why my husband would lie about that,' I say, shaking my head. 'But I do know this: Jace was right. I was run off the road yesterday by a man. He tried to kill me. My brakes were cut. And I think he must have been the one who cut Jace's brakes and caused his accident in April.'

'Chad Burrows,' Dawn says with disgust.

'Who is he?'

'Jace's former brother-in-law. Anne's brother.'

I'm shocked into silence. 'But why would he cut his own brother-in-law's brakes and put his sister in danger?'

Dawn shakes her head. 'It wasn't Chad that did it. He was in jail at the time. But I don't want to talk about him right now. I want to discuss Matt. And you.'

She takes another sip of tea. 'Would you like me to order you something? I don't drink alcohol, but they have a fully stocked bar if you'd like a wine or something stronger.'

'No. Thank you,' I say. 'When I met you for the first time that day at the restaurant, you had a champagne flute on your table. Were you drinking back then?'

She shakes her head and smiles. 'No. It's an old trick us zeros like to use. Sparkling water in a fancy glass.'

'So you met Matt online, in the AA group chat?'

She nods. At least he didn't lie to me about that.

'MorningBird83?' I ask.

Dawn nods again and sighs wearily. 'But there's a lot you don't know, Nadia.' She looks me in the eye.

'And it's about time you found out.'

32

I order a fresh pot of green tea for us to share and we settle into a more private corner of the lobby lounge so that we can speak privately.

'So it all started when I met Matt online. We connected right away. I was having issues in my marriage and Matt was depressed about his back. We both had our reasons for being miserable and as they say, misery loves company.'

'When exactly did you begin chatting?'

'At least a year ago. It was not long after Matt injured his back.'

Dawn stares down at her tea while she speaks. My heart thumps madly as I wait for her to admit that they had an affair. But what she says next surprises me.

'I love my husband. We have great chemistry and...' She pauses and her pale cheeks tint pink. 'As far as the bedroom goes, we were great in that department back then. But he didn't understand me. He always wanted to put a Band-Aid over my problems. Cover them up and act like they didn't exist. Pretend that I was still his perfect wife. But I wasn't. And our relationship wasn't enough for me anymore. That's where Matt came in.' She glances up at me.

'So you had an affair?' I ask.

'No. Not an affair. But he did fill the empty space in my heart that my husband couldn't fill. Matt became my best friend. We confided in each other like teenagers do.' She smiles. 'I've never had a best friend. I was always left out of the groups at school and used to eat my lunch in the library. Unlike Jace, who is... *was*, instantly liked by everyone who wandered into his orbit.' She plucks a tissue from her cardigan sleeve and dabs at her eyes.

'Jace had a good heart,' I say, thinking about what we did, what *he* did, so that I could walk away with the money that I was promised and so desperately needed. 'Right to the end.'

Dawn looks me in the eye.

'I know what Jace did for you. The money. The video.'

I blush and look away to stare out the window and admire a pretty fountain surrounded by a rose garden. The glimpses of blue ocean peeking through the garden walls calms me somehow, gives me strength.

'It's not something I'm proud of,' I say. 'But in the end Matthew got his operation and we were able to come and live here and avoid being homeless.'

'Matt told me about the eviction notice.' Dawn clears her throat. 'And that's when I stepped in with an olive branch.' She raises her palms. 'I'm not proud of myself, but my friend needed help and my brother Jace was going through his own troubles. So I stepped in and assisted them both.'

I sit up straighter in my seat. 'What do you mean?'

Dawn sighs. 'It's a lot to take in. But to cut it short, Jace had cheated on his wife with his receptionist at the time. Anne became enraged and she told her brother, Chad. Chad is a businessman who also has links with the underworld. He deals with the top three addictions: sex, drugs and money.' She shakes her head and curls her lips with disgust. 'He threatened Jace's life. Then he told him that if he was going to cheat on Anne, then he'd better make it worthwhile.'

'What do you mean?'

Chad runs a sex business. A porn website aimed at the rich. Their members sign up and pay a hefty fee and they can request particular kinks or scenes they'd like acted out in their porn videos, and his sex workers comply. A lot of money is made. The man is loaded.'

'Jace told me about that. But he said that a man named Joseph Stark ran it.'

'No. Joseph is employed by Chad. He's a nobody who just does what Chad says. Unfortunately, Jace lied to you. The whole thing – Joseph Stark making an offer on the house and then the upset neighbour souring the deal. It was all a set-up.'

'Chad started forcing Jace to sleep with his sex workers to make videos for his clients. But then one day, one of his top-tier clients, who used to be an estate agent for the rich and famous, requested something particularly specific. He wanted Jace to bed women, specifically non-sex workers, in the homes that he showed. To play out the role of a real estate agent banging his female clients to make a sale, which apparently is what the man used to do back in his day. He promised to pay top dollar for the videos, as long as normal, everyday women were used, not prostitutes. Apparently, he can tell the difference.' Dawn shudders.

I'm utterly shocked. 'So you being in the restaurant that day, that was also part of the set-up?'

Dawn nods.

'And it was Matt that told you where I'd be that day,' I say, shaking my head with disappointment.

'Yes.'

'So my husband basically pimped me out, is that what you're saying?'

'I'm so sorry, Nadia. He was so desperate for that operation. Not being able to work made him terribly insecure about your relationship. He was worried you'd leave him.'

I shake my head. 'So basically, my husband manipulated me, and with your help, steered me into the arms of your brother, who needed to sleep with me because he was being threatened by his screwed-up brother-in-law.'

'You were about to be evicted and forced to live in a car. Matthew couldn't see a way out.'

'Okay, I get that Matt was desperate, but he should have spoken to *me* about it, his wife, not some stranger on the internet.'

Dawn winces at my words.

'One question,' I say, frowning. 'Where did Jace get the money to pay me?'

'Chad Burrows. It was mostly dirty money. But this way it got washed through Jace's business. Jace had found some kind of a loophole. A way to claim the payments as client deposits. I'm not sure how it worked. But he was a clever man and he made it happen.'

'But why would Chad pay Jace if he hated him so much. Why not make him work for free?'

Dawn snorts. 'Trust me, you've never seen siblings as close as Chad and Anne. Jace and I used to call them Hansel and Gretel behind their backs.' She smiles at the memory, then sighs and grows serious. 'By making Jace work for him, it ensured that Anne would get to enjoy the benefits of her husband's extra income. Jace didn't get the money for himself. He had to transfer it into a separate account for Anne.' Dawn looks me in the eye. 'But Jace must have felt sorry for you. Because for the first time he used his own money from his savings account to pay you what he'd promised. He knew you needed it...' Dawn pauses to dab at her eyes again. 'Despite his faults, my brother always had a big heart.'

I reach out and lightly touch the back of Dawn's hand. 'I really am sorry about Jace. Even though I'm angry that he lied to me, I know deep down he was a good man.'

'Thank you,' Dawn says, her throat hoarse. 'It means a lot to hear that.'

'So why were you and Matt arguing at the fair this morning?'

Dawn's jaw tenses. 'Because he *lied* to me. Told me that Jace had never been to your house. But he had. And now he's dead.'

'Do you think Matt had something to do with it?'

'I'm not sure. That's what I want to find out. I need to know why Matt lied to me about Jace having been to your place.' She sets her cup down. 'I told the police about it. That he lied.'

I sit back against my chair and sigh. 'So that's why they've held him for questioning at the station.'

Dawn winces. 'I'm sorry about that.'

I shrug. 'Don't be. I'd want to know what happened to my brother if I had one.'

'Only child?'

I nod.

Dawn nods then sighs.

'You look exhausted. Maybe I should leave you to get some rest,' I say.

Dawn shakes her head. 'No. I need to speak with Matt. I need to know why he lied to me. There's something behind it. I'm sure of it.'

I think about that night and how I woke up to find Matt's side of the bed empty, and how I caught him coming in through the laundry door. What if he was disposing of Jace's body down at the rubbish tip? Could Chad have helped him? Is that how he knew that Jace was already dead? Does Matt know Chad?

'Come home with me,' I say. 'We can wait for Matt to be released by the police. Then we can both interrogate him at the same time.'

'I like the way you operate, Nadia.' Dawn smiles. 'I think, in another life, we might have been friends.'

'We still can be,' I say. 'It's never too late.

'For me it is,' Dawn says, her eyes shiny with emotion. 'I only have a year at most, maybe even less.'

I reach out and touch her hand again. 'I'm so sorry.'

'Don't be. I'll be with Jace again.' She blinks away her tears. 'But before then, I plan to spend my last days on earth fighting to put whoever did this to him behind bars.'

'And I want to help you do that. Let's go.'

After helping her out of the hotel and into the car, we hit the road and head for home. As soon as I turn onto my street, George comes running out from his property, as though he's been standing at the edge of his driveway waiting for me, waving his arms in the air.

'What now?' I mutter to myself, praying that there's no more bad news.

I wind down my window and George makes his way over.

'The cops have been looking for you. That constable – Laci I think – she wants to speak with you,' he says, his face grave. 'Said it's important. They dropped Mathew off at home then came straight here because he said he thought you might have come over to my place.'

I look at Dawn.

'I need to speak with Mathew,' she says. 'I can't wait another minute. You can drop me off at your house and then wait for me here if you like.'

'Annette's gone over to get him,' says George. 'She arrived back this morning.'

I look at George, puzzled. 'Annette? But she doesn't even know Matt. I don't think she's even met him yet.'

George shrugs. 'As soon as I told her that the police had dropped him off at home, she flew out the door like a woman on a mission and said it's not safe for him to be alone.'

I look at Dawn and then back at George. 'We're going home to see what's going on. But I promise we'll come back here after we've had a chance to speak with Matt.'

'Heck I'm getting too old for this,' George says, shaking his head. 'I'm going to call that constable to let her know that you're home.'

'That's a great idea. Thank you, George.'

He waves me off. 'Just stay safe and keep out of trouble.'

'Will do.'

I put the car into gear and drive the short distance to our place.

After I help Dawn out, I take her around the side of the house and let her in through the back door.

'Matt?' I call as we go inside.

It's strangely quiet, but there's an energy in the house. An unwelcome energy. As though the air is filled with static electricity.

I put a finger to my lips to signal Dawn to keep quiet, then I creep along the hallway and slowly take a peek around the wall so that I can see into the living room.

My heart stops.

Matt stands in the living room, facing me, and Annette is standing in front of him, her back to me, pointing a gun squarely at his face.

'I know you're there, Nadia. I can hear you.' She chuckles. 'If you don't want to see your husband's face blown off, you need to show yourself.'

Matt widens his eyes at me and indicates that I should run.

'Come out come out,' says Annette, the gun shaking in her hands.

I glance back at Dawn who indicates that I should enter with my hands up. Then she puts a finger to her lips and points to herself before retreating back into the laundry.

I take a deep breath and walk into the living room with my hands up.

'Don't shoot him,' I say, and come around to stand by Matt's side.

Annette moves the gun between us.

'None of you try anything funny. I know how to shoot a gun and you'll both end up dead.'

'What do you want from us?' I ask.

She laughs. 'Just your lives.'

'Why?'

'Because you took my husband from me, like all the others.'

'I don't even know you or your husband.'

'Well, aren't you slow,' Annette says. 'My husband is Jace... or was Jace. I'm Anne, his sad and pathetic estranged widow.'

I stare at her, dumbstruck. And then I see it. Replace the black hair with blond, the green eyes with blue, the pasty skin with a tan, and you have Jace's wife.

'But I thought you died in the car accident. It said in the newspaper that you'd died instantly.'

'That wasn't me.' Annette's... or *Anne's* mouth becomes a thin line. 'It was Jace's latest employee. They were on their way to Busselton to sell a highly priced property. A mansion on the beach. Sound familiar?'

I say nothing.

'So I made sure that they'd never make it to their destination. Mind you, I didn't know it was going to kill her. I was only hoping to ruin her pretty face.' She shrugs. 'But I felt so good after knowing that I'd ended her life, and I realised that I wouldn't feel satisfied until I'd killed you all off. Every woman Jace had ever cheated on me with.'

'It wasn't cheating though. I needed the money. It was a business transaction. Jace and I had no feelings towards each other apart from being work colleagues.'

'Sure. That's why I caught him watching your video the day after he returned home.'

I'm not sure how I feel about this. Humiliation. For both myself and for Anne.

'You don't want to do this, Annette– Anne. If there's anyone to blame, it's your brother, Chad. He was holding your husband ransom. And he tried to kill me.'

'That's because I asked him to,' she says, snapping.

I shuffle closer to Matt and take his hand in mine. He grips my fingers tightly, his palms sweaty. He's as scared as I am.

'Now, who should I shoot first?' Anne asks pointing the gun at me, then Matt, me then Matt.

Just when I'm about to lose hope, Dawn rises behind Annette, her hand wrapped around my cat statue from the laundry. I try my best not to react and to keep my eyes focussed on Anne.

'Jace loved you, Anne,' I say. 'He did those things for your brother because he loved *you*. Otherwise he would have just walked away from your marriage. But he didn't.'

Anne swallows thickly and her eyes well with tears.

'I don't care about Jace,' she says. 'He's dead now and I'm the one who made sure of it.'

'You killed him?' I ask. I don't dare look at Dawn.

'After your husband chased him away from your house that night, it was easy. My brother was the one who snapped his neck, by the way. But I was the one who drove his body to the tip. My brother didn't want to dirty his new car.' She laughs.

My blood runs cold. This woman is completely crazy.

'And now it's your turn to join Jace,' Anne says.

She aims her gun at me just as Dawn raises her arm and swings the ceramic cat down hard against the back of Anne's head.

The statue shatters and Anne collapses to the ground. She's not unconscious but she's been hit hard enough for Matt to wrestle the gun out of her hand. He pins her to the floor and passes the gun to me. I take the thing outside, with outstretched arms, and sit it on the lawn where it's well out of reach.

Dawn stares down at Anne, who appears dazed. Tears flow frow freely down Dawn's cheeks. 'That was for my brother, you evil bitch.'

Police sirens sound. I sigh with relief and hug Dawn before carefully steering her to the couch. She must have given that hit everything she had.

'Can I get you anything?'

Dawn shakes her head. 'I just want a good rest,' she says, her lids fluttering closed. 'I'm so tired.'

I carefully wedge some soft pillows around her and drape a blanket across her legs.

Swifty appears from out of nowhere and jumps onto Dawn's lap. She scratches around the blanket until she settles herself and curls up into a ball. Dawn strokes Swifty's fur and smiles with her eyes closed. Swifty trills in response.

'I love cats,' she whispers.

The police burst in through the back door and take over from Matt. Constable Laci drags Anne to her feet and slaps handcuffs on her wrists.

'You are arrested for murder, and for the concealment of the murder victim's body.'

33

Constable Small is the one who drives Anne away to the station, to where they already have Chad Burrows arrested for Jace's murder. Constable Laci hangs back to speak with me.

'Alone,' she says, her eyes on Matt.

'Let me tell her myself,' Matt says. 'It's my mistake. I need to be the one to own up to it.'

Constable Laci folds her arms across her chest. 'Okay. But I'm going to stay here until you do. Just to make sure you tell her the truth.'

Matt sighs. 'Be my guest. But can we at least have a little bit of privacy?'

Constable Laci nods. 'I'm going to make myself a coffee. You've got a nice machine.' She enters the kitchen where George is making himself a cup of tea, and a green tea for Dawn, who is now resting in the guest bedroom.

Matt and I sit down together on the couch in the living room, a large space between us.

'This is going to be difficult to hear,' Matt says, eyeing me nervously. 'It's hard to say too.' He cracks his knuckles and whistles through his teeth.

'Just tell me, Matt. We need to be truthful to each other from now on.'

'It's not that easy, trust me. I've been a dick of a husband.'

'You think?'

Matt's face remains dead serious.

'This is going to blow your mind. In a bad way. You're going to be more than upset. In fact, I don't think you'll ever want to speak to me again.'

Anger and resentment flares up inside of me. He's going to tell me about how he set me up with Jace. How he is the one responsible for involving me in this mess.

'Will you just tell me?'

He nods and sighs deeply.

'You know the stalker you had? The guy who was sending you lingerie and weird messages?'

'Tell her everything,' Constable Laci shouts from the kitchen.

'I am trying to,' Matt says. He exhales. 'The guy who made the fake Instagram account with all your old photos on there?'

'Yes...' I frown in confusion. 'What about him?'

'It was me.'

I blink and wait for Matt to chuckle and say that he's joking. But he doesn't. He just sits there and looks like he's about to cry.

'What do you mean? Why are you saying this?'

Matt rakes a hand through his hair and groans with frustration. 'Because it was me. There was never a stalker.'

I stare at him, open mouthed. 'Why on earth would you do that?'

He shrugs. 'Because it made you need me again. I felt so useless after the accident, and I could see that you viewed me differently. Then I was watching a daytime movie one day while you were out and I got the idea. I thought that if you I scared you a little, you wouldn't leave me. I did it out of love. You need to understand that. Only because I love you so much.'

He reaches for my hand but I slide it out of reach.

'I'm not sure that I can get past this, Matt. Along with setting me up with Jace to get the money for your operation, I'm not sure that I can ever trust you again.'

'But I got cold feet on the day of the interview. I tried to stop you.'

'What are you talking about?'

'That morning of your job interview, with Jace, I tried to stop you. I couldn't handle the idea of you with another man.'

'Okay. I do remember that. But once I got the job, you had plenty of time to stop me. You could have stopped me before I left with Jace for Busselton. But you didn't.' I shake my head and my chest tightens at the memory. 'All those excited messages and emojis you were sending me. You wrote those texts knowing I was going to have to sleep with another man for money.'

Matt sighs and hangs his head. 'I know. And I'll never forgive myself for it.'

Someone knocks on the front door and George goes to answer it. A few seconds later, Misha walks in. I leap off the couch and run up to give her a huge hug.

'Oh my god,' she says, when she sees all the people in the house. 'What happened? I knew something was up when I couldn't get through to your number.'

I pull out my phone, confused. 'But you haven't called me.'

She takes my phone and brings up her contact and shakes her head. 'It says that you've blocked me.'

'But I didn't,' I say.

We both look at Matt, who gets up off the couch and raises his palms. 'Okay, it was me. And I'm sorry. I was just afraid you were going to run away to Albany.'

'Wow. I can't listen to this anymore,' I say, and walk over to Constable Laci, who is sipping her coffee out of a cat-shaped mug and watching us all like we're a daytime soap.

'Am I allowed to leave town now?' I ask her. 'Because I want to go to Albany with my friend,' I say, nodding at Mischa.

'Nadia,' says Matt. 'Think this through first. Come on. Don't leave me like this.'

'You know you can press charges for the stalking,' Constable Laci says.

I look at Matt, who's cradling his head in his hands. 'Let me think about it. I need time.'

'Fair enough. You've got my number,' she says.

I leave her chatting with Misha while I go pack. Then I bring the carrier out and put Swifty inside.

'You can't take the cat. She was my nan's pet,' Matt says angrily.

I look at him and raise my brows. 'Really? Who feeds her and cleans her litter each day? And don't you think you owe me?'

He shakes his head and sighs noisily. 'You know what? Whatever. Just go.'

'Don't worry, I will,' I say, more harshly than I intend. But deep inside, my heart is breaking. When I took my vows with Matt on our wedding day, I meant them, with every part of me.

Misha helps me to load the car with Swifty's food, her toys, and her litter bags, as well as my clothes. Then we go back inside so that I can say my goodbyes to everyone.

Constable Laci makes me promise to keep in touch and to let her know how I'm doing in Albany once I get settled in, and George asks me to do the same. I give him a huge hug and thank him for everything. I tell him that I'll keep my promise about fixing his wife's car.

'Don't worry about the car,' he says. 'It'll give me something to do.' He also promises he'll keep an eye on Matt and will make sure to check on him from time to time.

I head to the guest bedroom and knock softly on the door.

'Come in,' Dawn says weakly.

I inhale deeply in order to calm myself before entering. After speaking with Matt, all the hurt feels raw. I'm not sure that I'll ever get over the fact that Matt and Dawn set me up to make a porn video – a video that can never be erased.

But when I see her on the bed, as pale and fragile as a wilted flower, I can't help but soften my heart towards her.

'How are you feeling?' I ask.

'Better now that I know Hansel and Gretel are going to be behind bars for a long time.'

I smile. 'I'm actually leaving town. I'm going to stay with my best friend in Albany.'

'Good for you,' Dawn says. 'You deserve to be happy.'

'We all do,' I say. I sit down on the edge of her bed.

'Maybe I'll come to see you one day,' she says, her dark eyes – so like Jace's eyes – shiny with tears.

'I'd like that,' I tell her, my throat tightening.

'My husband is driving down as we speak to come and get me,' she says. 'He's upset that I took off while he was visiting his mother.'

'I'm sure he won't stay mad at you when he finds out you were the hero and saved the day.'

'Oh please,' she says, waving my words away. She grows serious and shakes her head. 'I'm truly sorry for all the hurt I caused you, Nadia. It was awful of me.'

'I know.' I blink back the tears that burn my eyes. 'And I accept your apology. I think you more than made up for it by saving our lives. I'll be forever grateful to you, and I'm sure Matt will be too.'

'He loves you,' she says, softly.

'I know. But I'm not sure that's the kind of love that I want.'

'Fair enough. Good luck, Nadia.'

'Good luck to you too, Dawn.' I get to my feet and give her a smile. Then I turn and walk out, gently closing the door behind me.

'Are you ready?' asks Misha, when I enter the kitchen.

'Yes,' I say, exhaling. 'I think so.'

Everyone gathers to see us out, including Matt.

Swifty is quiet in her carrier. I'm surprised she's not traumatised by the last time she was in it. But there are hidden treats in the folds of the blanket that will keep her occupied for a while.

I climb into the passenger seat of Misha's car and Matt comes to the window, which I wind down.

'Goodbye, Nadia,' he says. 'Let me know when you get there safely.'

'I will,' I say, a lump growing in my throat.

Thankfully Misha starts the car before I begin to bawl, and we lurch into gear and slowly start driving away.

George, Matt and Constable Laci wave. I wave back and continue to do so until they disappear from view. I have tears streaming down my cheeks.

'Why is it so hard to let go of someone, even when they aren't good for you?' I say, wiping my eyes with the backs of my hands.

'Story of my life,' says Misha, grinning. We laugh.

Her face grows serious. 'I'm sorry though, that you went through all of... whatever it was that happened. I think we're going to need to open up a bottle of wine as soon as we get home, because I get the feeling you have a lot to unpack, both mentally and physically.'

'That sounds nice. Not the rehashing everything part. But the wine.'

She giggles. 'Now you're sounding more like yourself. God, I've missed you.'

'I've missed you too. And guess what?'

'What?'

'I've kept my promise. I'm coming to your birthday weekend after all.'

Swifty meows from the back seat and I turn to her and reach out and stroke her fur through the mesh. 'It's okay, sweetie. We're going to be safe now.'

'You can stay for as long as you like, by the way,' says Misha. 'Forever if you need to.'

'Thanks,' I say. 'But I think after a good rest I'm going to return home. Find a place in South Fremantle by the beach and just enjoy the small things. Sunsets and hot chips after a swim in the ocean. Hot coffee in the early mornings.' I lean my head out of the car and watch the trees passing by. 'I can continue my baking thing. Really throw myself into it and try to turn it into a proper business.'

'Good for you. I can really see that happening, you know. I can picture it. And I can picture you happy, too.'

I smile and stare at the afternoon sunlight dappling the open road.

'So can I.'

The End

If you enjoyed this book, please let others know by leaving a quick review on Amazon. Also, if you spot anything untoward in the paperback, get in touch. We strive for the best quality and appreciate reader feedback.

editor@thebookfolks.com

Also by Vanessa Garbin

WHAT WE DID LAST NIGHT

When a group of close friends decide to hold a partner-swapping key party one night, it is meant to be "just a bit of fun". No obligations, but no strings attached. And anything that does happen will remain under wraps. But things quickly start to unravel, with utterly deadly consequences.

THE LIES I TOLD HIM

When Daphne's teenage son returns from a party, distraught, he refuses to tell his mother what's up. But someone has filmed him in a compromising situation with a girl, and they are using it to get what they want. As Daphne tries to solve the problem, her own past comes back to haunt her and place everything she holds dear in jeopardy.

YOUR EVERY MOVE

When young mother Dana discovers a bag of money under a bush, she thinks her problems may be over. Unfortunately, they are only just beginning. She starts to receive letters from someone claiming to be her "number one fan" and unless she complies with their bizarre demands, her family will be in danger.

THE STEPS WE TAKE

A mother becomes increasingly at odds with her local community when she tries to deal with the bullying of her daughter at school. Yet her daughter is trying to handle it in her own way. When one bullying schoolboy goes missing, the family will have to reach the truth to remain together.

THEIR LITTLE SECRETS

Sara's marriage is already under strain when her best friend's daughter disappears. With the parents acting strange, and her husband absent-minded and evasive, Sara starts suspecting they share a secret. When the body of a girl is found in a lake nearby, her resolve to solve the mystery will force her to question everyone she thought she knew.

NO FRIENDS OF MINE

Marilyn is at a low point, so when she receives an invitation to holiday with some old friends, she doesn't think she has much to lose. But old friends bring with them old memories, in particular those of a terrible event that happened ten years ago. As the past is dug up, having been bored with her life, Marilyn will now find herself fighting for it.

FOR MY OWN GOOD

Mary is on meds which make her forgetful. It's been like this ever since an incident when their baby was injured. Now her husband is being way over-protective. He insists Mary stays indoors, for her own good. He's hired a nanny. But Mary can't remember her child getting hurt. And if she can't recall what happened, how can she make things right?

LIES WITHIN ME

After being taken speed-dating by her friends, Alice wakes up in a stranger's house. She can't remember the night before, but thinks she has been drugged and assaulted. Worse, however, is the man responsible is found murdered. Was it her? If not, who killed him? Finding the culprit might be the only way to get herself out of the frame.

FREE with Kindle Unlimited and available in paperback!

Other titles of interest

CATFISH by Sadie Norman

It is not without some malice that rookie detective Anna McArthur is called "crazy" by her colleagues. She certainly tends to act first and think later. But when Anna discovers the body of a murdered woman who has "catfish" carved into her chest, she feels a personal duty to do everything she can to up her game and find the killer.

FREE with Kindle Unlimited and available in paperback!

LASTING INFLUENCE by Linda Hagan

When two social media influencers are kidnapped, DCI Gawn Girvin is called back from extended leave to investigate. One of the abductees is the son of the Norwegian Ambassador, and the powers that be want the matter sorted quickly. Yet Gawn's search for the couple will lead her to places that intersect with her own troubled past.

FREE with Kindle Unlimited and available in paperback!

Printed in Great Britain
by Amazon

49114959R00111